'I don't believe this!'  **incredulo** **seriously as** **just to solv** **problems?'**

'Why not? You're .... said Mal.

'And what do I get out of this deal?'

Mal looked at her in surprise. 'I would have thought that was obvious. You get the chance to run your business at Birraminda.'

'It's a big step from administrator to wife,' Copper pointed out, still hardly able to credit that they were actually *talking* about the crazy idea.

'You don't have to be madly in love to work successfully with someone.'

'No, but it helps when you're married to them! Can we get this quite clear? You'll let Copley Travel use Birraminda if I agree to marry you, but if not, the whole project's off?'

'That's it,' Mal agreed, as if pleased with her quick comprehension.

Jessica Hart had a haphazard career before she began writing to finance a degree in history. Her experience ranged from waitress, theatre production assistant and outback cook to newsdesk secretary, expedition PA and English teacher, and she has worked in countries as different as France and Indonesia, Australia and Cameroon. She now lives in the north of England, where her hobbies are limited to eating and drinking and travelling when she can, preferably to places where she'll find good food or desert or tropical rain.

Recent titles by the same author:

KISSING SANTA
BRIDE FOR HIRE

OUTBACK BRIDE

BY
JESSICA HART

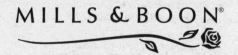

First published in Great Britain 1997
Harlequin Mills & Boon Limited,
Eton House, 18-24 Paradise Road, Richmond, Surrey TW9 1SR

© Jessica Hart 1997

ISBN 0 263 80411 9

Set in Times Roman 10½ on 12 pt.
02-9710-53755 C1

Printed and bound in Great Britain
by Mackays of Chatham PLC, Chatham

CHAPTER ONE

'HELLO?' The door stood open behind its fly screen. Copper peered through, but could make out only a long, dim corridor lined with boots, coats and an assortment of riding gear. 'Hello?' she called again. 'Is there anyone there?'

No response. She could hear her voice echoing in the empty house and glanced at her watch. Nearly four o'clock. You'd think there would be *someone* around. Her father had mentioned a housekeeper. Shouldn't she be here, keeping house instead of leaving it open for any passing stranger?

Not that there would be many passing strangers out here. Copper turned and looked out to where her car was parked in the full glare of an outback afternoon. A dusty track had brought her from beyond the horizon to this long, low homestead with its deep verandah and its corrugated iron roof that flashed in the sun, and here it stopped. Talk about the end of the road.

Still, this was just what their clients would want to see, Copper reassured herself: a gracious colonial homestead at the centre of a vast cattle station, accessible only by plane or fifty miles of dirt track.

Copper adjusted her sunglasses on her nose and looked around her with a touch of impatience. It was frustrating to have got this far and not be able to get straight down to business.

She paced up and down the verandah, wondering how long she would have to wait for Matthew Standish and what he would be like. Her father had just said that he was 'nobody's fool' and that she would have to handle him with care. Copper intended to. The future of Copley Travel depended on Matthew Standish agreeing to let them use Birraminda as a base for their new luxury camping tours, and she wasn't going to go home until she had that agreement signed and dated.

She looked at her watch again. Where was everybody? Copper hated hanging around waiting for things to happen; she liked to make them happen herself. Crossly, she sat down on the top step, very conscious of the silence settling around her, broken only by the mournful caw of a raven somewhere down by the creek. She would hate to live anywhere this quiet.

This was Mal's kind of country. She remembered how he had talked about the outback, about its stillness and its silence and its endless empty horizons. It was easy to imagine him out here, rangy and unhurried, beneath the pitiless blue sky.

Copper frowned. She wished she could forget about Mal. He belonged to the past, and she was a girl who liked to live in the present and look to the future. She had thought she had done a good job of filing his memory away as something secret and special, to be squirrelled away and taken out only when she was alone or down and wanted to remember that, however unromantic she might be, she too had had her moment of magic, but the long drive through the interior had inevitably reminded her of him. His image was out, like a genie from its lamp, and just as impossible to bottle up and ignore.

It wasn't even as if she had ever believed in love at first sight. Copper was the last person who had expected to meet a stranger's eyes and know that her life had changed for ever, and yet that was how it had been. Almost corny.

She had been at the centre of the crowd, as usual, and Mal had been on the edge, a solitary man but not a lonely one. He had a quality of quiet assurance that set him apart from everyone else on the beach, and when he had looked up, and their eyes had met, it was as if every love song ever composed had been written especially for her...

Copper sighed. Three warm Mediterranean nights, that was all they had had. Three nights, on the other side of the world, more than seven years ago. You would think she would have forgotten him by now.

Only he hadn't been the kind of man you could ever forget.

'Hello.'

Jerked out of the past by the unexpected voice behind her, Copper swivelled round from her seat on the steps. She found herself being regarded by a little girl who had come round the corner of the verandah and was staring at her with the frank, unsettling gaze of a child. She had a tangle of dark curls, huge blue eyes and a stubborn, wilful look. A beautiful child, Copper thought, or she would have been if she hadn't been quite so grubby. Her dungarees were torn and dirty and her small face was smeared with dust.

'You made me jump!' she said.

The little girl just carried on staring. 'What's your name?' she demanded.

'Copper,' said Copper.

The blue eyes darkened suspiciously. 'Copper's not a real name!'

'Well, no,' she admitted. 'It's a nickname—it's what

my friends call me.' Seeing that the child looked less than convinced, she added hastily, 'What's *your* name?'

'Megan. I'm four and a half.'

'I'm twenty seven and three quarters,' offered Copper.

Megan considered this, and then, as if satisfied, she came along the verandah and sat down on the top step next to Copper, who glanced down at the tousled head curiously. Her father hadn't mentioned anything about a child. Come to think of it, he had been so taken up with the beauty of the property that he hadn't said much at all about the people who lived there. All she knew was that Birraminda had a formidable owner. Perhaps it might be easier to start with the owner's wife?

'Is your mother around?' she asked Megan, hoping to find someone she could introduce herself to properly while she waited for Matthew Standish to appear.

Megan looked at her as if she was stupid. 'She's dead.'

'Oh, dear,' said Copper inadequately, thrown as much by the matter-of-fact little voice as by the information. What *did* you say to a child who had lost its mother? 'That's very sad. I'm sorry, Megan. Er…who looks after you?'

'Kim does.'

The housekeeper? 'Where's Kim now?' she asked.

'She's gone.'

'Gone?' echoed Copper, taken aback. What was this place, the *Marie Celeste*? 'Gone where?'

'I don't know,' Megan admitted. 'But Dad was cross with Uncle Brett because now there's no one to look after me.'

Copper's heart was wrung as she looked down at the oddly self-possessed little girl beside her. Poor little mite! Had she been abandoned entirely? She opened her mouth to ask the child if there was anyone who knew where she was when a voice called Megan's name, and the next moment a man came round the corner of the homestead from the direction of the old woolshed.

He was tall and lean, that much Copper could see, but in his stockman's hat, checked shirt, jeans and dusty boots he looked, at a distance, just like any other outback man. And yet there was something about him, something about the easy, unhurried way he moved, that clutched at Copper's throat. For a heart-stopping moment he reminded her so vividly of Mal that she felt quite breathless, and could only stare across the yard to where he had checked at the sight of her.

It couldn't be Mal, she told herself as she struggled to breathe normally. She was being ridiculous. Mal belonged to the past, to Turkey and a few star-shot nights. It was just the outback playing tricks with her mind. She had been thinking about him so much over the last few days that now she was going to imagine that every man she met was him. This man just happened to have the same air of quiet strength. It didn't mean he was Mal.

And then he moved out of the shadow of the house and came towards the steps to stand looking up at where she sat next to Megan, and Copper found herself getting shakily to her feet, her heart drumming in disbelief.

It couldn't be Mal, but it was…it *was*! No one else could have that quiet mouth or those unfathomable brown eyes, steady and watchful beneath the dark brows. No other man could have just that angle of cheek and jaw, or make her bones dissolve just by standing there.

Would he remember her as clearly as she remembered him? Oh, God, what if he did? Or would it be worse if he *didn't*?

Beneath his hat, Mal's eyes narrowed as he looked up

at Copper, clinging to the verandah post as if her legs
were too weak to support her. She was wearing loose
shorts and a matching short-sleeved linen jacket, an outfit she had chosen with care to impress the formidable
Mr Standish. In the motel that morning it had seemed to
strike the perfect balance between casual elegance and
practicality, but the long, bumpy drive since then had
left her looking instead hot, crumpled and ridiculously
out of place, and the wavy brown hair that normally
swung in a blunt cut to her jaw was dusty and limp.

All too conscious of the picture she must make,
Copper was passionately grateful for the sunglasses that
hid her eyes. Swallowing convulsively, she managed a
weak 'hello', although her voice sounded so high and
tight that she hardly recognised it as her own.

Before Mal had a chance to reply, Megan had
launched herself down the steps towards him. 'Dad!'

Copper's mind, still spinning with shock, jarred to a
sickening halt. *Dad?* All those times she had wondered
about Mal and what he was doing, not once had she
pictured him as a husband, as a father. And yet, why
not? He must be thirty five by now, quite old enough to
have settled down with a wife and child. It was just that
he had been such a solitary man, Copper told herself,
pretending that the hollow feeling in her stomach was
due simply to surprise.

It was hard to imagine anyone so self-contained
bogged down in a life of domesticity, that was all. Surely
that was reason enough for her to feel as if someone had
hit her very hard in the solar plexus? It had nothing
whatsoever to do with any silly dreams that he might
have stayed faithful to the memory of the few short days
they had spent together. She hadn't, so why should he?

Mal had caught Megan instinctively as she hurtled

down the steps, and now swung her up into his arms. 'I thought I told you to stay on the fence where I could see you?' he said to her, but spoilt the stern effect by ruffling her dark curls before lowering her to the ground once more. Megan hung onto his hand as he turned his attention back to Copper, his expression quite unreadable.

'At last,' he said unexpectedly. 'I've been waiting for you.'

For one extraordinary moment Copper thought that he was telling her that he'd waited seven years for her after all. 'For—for *me*?' she stuttered, trying not to stare.

The angular face was just as she remembered, cool, rather quiet, but with strong, well-defined features and a mouth which could look almost stern in repose but which could relax too into an unexpected smile. Copper had never forgotten that smile, how it transformed his whole face and how the air had evaporated from her lungs the first time she had seen it.

He wasn't smiling now. The years had etched harsher lines around his mouth and there was a shuttered look to his eyes. Copper thought he looked tired, and her shock was punctured at last by shame as she remembered that Megan's mother was dead. It was no wonder that he looked harder, older than her memory.

'You're late,' Mal was saying, apparently unaware of her inner turmoil. 'I was expecting you at least four days ago.'

Had her father given him an exact date to expect her when he had written? Copper looked puzzled, but before she could ask him what he meant Megan had tugged at his hand. 'Her name's Copper.'

There was a tiny moment of silence. Surely he must remember her name, if nothing else, Copper thought wildly. She had sunglasses on and her hair was quite different now, but her name hadn't changed. She waited for Mal to turn, recognition and surprise lighting his face, but he was looking down at his daughter.

'Copper?' he repeated, his voice empty of all expression.

'It's not a proper name,' Megan informed him. 'It's a nickname.'

Mal did look at Copper then, but his brown eyes were quite unreadable. Could it be that he really *had* forgotten her? An obscure sense of pique sharpened Copper's voice.

'I'm Caroline Copley,' she said, relieved to hear that she sounded almost her old business-like self. At least her voice had lost that humiliating squeak. 'I was hoping to see Matthew Standish.'

'I'm Matthew Standish,' said Mal calmly, and all her newly recovered poise promptly deserted her as her jaw dropped.

'*You* are? But—' She broke off in embarrassment.

Mal lifted an eyebrow. 'But what?'

What could she say? She could hardly accuse him of not knowing his own name, and if she did she would have to explain how they had met before. Copper had her pride, and she was damned if she was going to remind a man that he had once made love to her!

She didn't remember telling him about her name, or asking him about his own. He might have told her his surname, but if he had, she hadn't remembered it. She remembered only his slow, sure hands on her skin and the strange sense of coming home as she had walked barefoot across the sand towards him.

'But what?' said Mal again. He didn't remember her. *He* wasn't racked by memories. His heart wasn't booming in his ears at the thought of what they had once shared. He was just standing there with that inscrutable look on his face, waiting for a flustered stranger to answer his question.

'Nothing,' said Copper. Realising that she was still clinging to the verandah post, she let it go hurriedly. 'I mean, I…I was expecting an older man, that's all.'

'I'm sorry to disappoint you.' Was that an undercurrent of amusement in his voice? 'If it's any comfort, you're not exactly what I was expecting either.'

His face didn't change, there wasn't even a suspicion of a smile about his mouth, but somehow Copper got the feeling that he was laughing at her. Confused, uncertain whether to feel hurt or relieved that Mal didn't remember her, she stuck her chin out. 'Oh?' she said almost belligerently. 'What were you expecting me to be like?'

Mal studied her with a disconcerting lack of haste, from her flushed face, tense and vivid beneath her sunglasses, down over the slender figure in the crumpled suit, down slim, brown legs to the leather sandals which showed off deep red toenails. Still standing nervously at the top of the steps, Copper managed to look tired and vibrant and completely out of place.

'Let's say that I was expecting someone a little more…practical,' he said at last.

'I'm very practical,' snapped Copper, burningly aware of his scrutiny.

Mal said nothing, but his eyes rested on her toenails and she had to resist the urge to curl up her feet. He obviously thought she was just a city girl who had no idea about life in the outback. City girl she might be, but impractical she wasn't. She was a professional businesswoman and it was about time she behaved like one, instead of stuttering and stammering like a school-girl just because she had come face to face with a man she had met briefly more than seven years ago. It was a surprise, a coincidence, but no more than that.

Mal's unspoken disbelief helped Copper pull herself together. 'I realise I don't look quite as efficient as I usually do,' she said coldly, 'but it was a longer drive than I anticipated, and your track is in very poor condition.'

'You should have come in the bus,' said Mal, with a disparaging glance across to where her car sat, looking as citified and inappropriate as she did. 'I'd have sent someone to pick you up.'

Copper eyed him in some puzzlement. Her father had written to say that his daughter would be coming to Birraminda to negotiate the deal in his stead, but she certainly hadn't had the impression that Matthew Standish had been so enthusiastic about their plan that he would go to the trouble of collecting her. Still, per-haps her father had misjudged his interest?

'I thought it would be better for me to be independ-ent,' she said loftily, unprepared for the look of distaste that swept across Mal's face.

'We've had enough independent types at Birraminda,' he said in a flat voice. 'And it's not as if you're going to need a car while you're here.' His mouth twisted with sudden bitterness. 'I'm reliably informed that there's no-where to go.'

Looking out at the empty horizon, Copper could be-lieve it. 'Well, no,' she agreed. 'But I wasn't planning on staying for ever!'

An odd look flickered in Mal's eyes and then was gone. 'I realise that,' he said expressionlessly. He looked down at the child leaning trustfully against his leg, and rested his hand on the small head. 'I can't say I'm not glad to see you, anyway,' he added as if he had just reminded himself of something. 'Megan, run along and tell Uncle Brett to finish off without me, will you?'

Megan nodded importantly and scampered off. Mal looked after her, his expression unguarded for a moment, and, watching him, Copper felt something twist inside her. He had looked at her like that once. She suppressed a sigh as he turned back to her, his face closed once more. She might as well forget all about their brief affair right now. Mal obviously had.

'You'd better come inside,' he said, climbing up the steps towards her and Copper found herself taking a quick step back in case he brushed against her.

Her instinctive movement didn't go unnoticed by Mal. He made no comment, and his eyes were as inscrutable as ever, but Copper was convinced there was subtle mockery in the way he held the screen door open for her, as if he knew just how confused she was, how terrified that his slightest touch would bring back an avalanche of memories.

Head held high, she walked past him into the house. Inside, all was dim and cool and quiet. The homestead was much bigger than Copper had imagined from outside, with several corridors leading off from the long entrance hall, and it had a kind of dusty charm that she had somehow not expected to find this far from any kind of civilisation.

Mal led the way along to a very large, very untidy kitchen with a door onto the back verandah. Through the window, Copper could see a dusty yard shaded by a gnarled old gum and surrounded by a collection of outbuildings, a tall windmill and two enormous iron water tanks. To one side lay the creek, where cockatoos wheeled out of the trees and galahs darted over the water, turning in flashes of pink and grey, and in the distance an irrigated paddock looked extraordinarily green and lush compared to the expanse of bare holding yards that stretched out of sight. Copper could just make out some cattle milling around in the pens, lifting clouds of red dust with their hooves.

Tossing his hat onto the table, Mal crossed over to the sink and filled up the kettle. 'Tea?'

'Er…yes…thank you.' Copper took off her sunglasses and sank down into a chair. She felt very odd.

At times, perhaps more often than she wanted to admit, she had dreamt about meeting Mal again. Her fantasies had usually involved them catching sight of each other unexpectedly, their faces lighting up with instant recognition. Sometimes she had pictured him shouldering his way through crowds towards her, reaching for her hands, surrendering to the same electric attraction that had brought them together the first night they met. Or she had let herself imagine him looking deep into her eyes and explaining how he had lost her address and spent the last seven years scouring England and Australia to find her again.

What she *hadn't* imagined was that he would behave as if he had never seen her before in his life and calmly offer her a cup of tea!

Copper sighed inwardly. Perhaps it was just as well. She mustn't forget that she was here to set up a vital deal, and trying to negotiate with a man who remembered the past as clearly as she did would have been more than a little awkward.

Her clear green eyes rested on Mal's back as he made tea in a battered enamel pot. The sureness of his every gesture tugged at her heart. Her gaze drifted from the broad shoulders down to lean hips, and she was suddenly swamped with the memory of how it had felt to run her hands over him. It was as if she could still feel the texture of his skin beneath her fingers, still trace the outline of his spine and feel his muscles flex in response to her touch.

Memory pulsated like pain in her fingertips, and Copper drew a sharp breath and squeezed her eyes shut. She opened them just as Mal turned round, and across the kitchen their gazes locked.

Copper wanted to look away, to make a light comment and laugh, but she couldn't move. She was riveted by the current of awareness that leapt to life between them, held by those deep, deep brown eyes while her heart began to boom and thud in her ears. Why had she taken her sunglasses off? She felt naked and vulnerable without them. Her eyes had always been embarrassingly transparent. One look into them and Mal would know that her hands were still tingling with the memory of his body, that all those years, when he had forgotten her, his kisses had continued to haunt her dreams.

Then Mal moved forward and set the teapot down on the table, and Copper jerked her eyes away with a tiny gasp. He looked at her narrowly. 'Are you all right?'

'I'm fine,' said Copper, horribly conscious of how high and tight her voice sounded. She could feel the telltale colour blotching her throat and willed it to fade. 'I'm just a bit tired, that's all.'

Mal pulled out a chair and sat down opposite her. 'You wouldn't be tired if you'd taken the bus,' he said, pouring the tea into two mugs.

Copper sat up straighter at the implied criticism. She had, in fact, looked into doing the journey on the bus in case they wanted to offer it as option to their clients, but it would have taken forty-eight hours just to get to the nearest town—hardly a recipe for arriving fresh as a daisy! 'Oh, wouldn't I?' she retorted. 'How long is it since *you've* been on a bus?'

'Not for years.' An intriguing half-smile dented the corners of Mal's mouth as he acknowledged her point. 'Now you come to mention it, I don't think I've been on a bus since I was travelling in Europe—a long time ago now.'

Seven years. For one awful moment, Copper thought she had spoken aloud, but a covert look at Mal showed that he was calmly drinking his tea. He looked cool and self-contained, a little watchful, perhaps, but certainly not like a man who had suddenly been brought face to face with embarrassment from the past. What would he say if she told him that she knew exactly when he had been in Europe? Oh, yes, she could have said. I remember you then. We spent three days making love on a beach.

Great way to impress him with her professionalism.

'Oh,' she said weakly instead.

She risked another glance at Mal, who was looking thoughtfully down into his tea, dark brows drawn together as if pondering an insuperable problem. Copper could see the lines of strain around his eyes and she wondered how long ago his wife had died. What had she been like, the woman who had shared his life and borne his child? All at once Copper was ashamed of herself for worrying about the past and whether Mal remembered her or not. He had more important things to think about than a girl he had met on a beach seven years ago.

And, really, wasn't that all it had been? A chance encounter, ships passing in the night? It had felt much more than that at the time, but it was all so long ago and they were different people now. Mal had changed and so had she. All she had to do was forget about that brief, magical interlude and pretend that he was a complete stranger.

Easy.

It didn't stop her heart lurching when Mal looked up suddenly from his tea and found her watching him, but at least this time she was able to look away. 'What...what a nice kitchen,' she said brightly. It was the first thing that came into her head, but when she looked at it, it *was* a nice kitchen, cool and spacious and beautifully designed, although most of the equipment was hidden beneath a clutter of packets and jars, papers and unwashed dishes.

'I'm sorry about the mess,' said Mal, as if he had read her mind. He looked ruefully around him. 'This is a busy time on the station and everything's got out of control in the house since Kim left. We really need a good housekeeper to sort everything out.'

'I can see that,' said Copper with feeling, averting her eyes from the dirty dishes piled high in the sink. She wasn't obsessively tidy herself, but her business brain deplored the inefficiency.

'Have you spent any time in the outback before?' asked Mal abruptly, and Copper set down her mug. She had a feeling that some kind of interview was just beginning.

'Not really,' she said cautiously. Her father had warned her that Mal had been unimpressed by the idea of a city firm setting up luxury camping trips, so it would be up to her to convince him that they knew what they were doing. 'A couple of camping trips in the Flinders Ranges, that's all.'

Mal sighed. 'In other words, you don't have any relevant experience?'

'I wouldn't say that,' said Copper rather coldly. There was no need for him to write her off just yet! She had been organising tours for more than five years and it wasn't as if she was going to be leading the groups herself. Her role was strictly administrative. 'I don't need to be Crocodile Dundee, do I?' she added with a challenging look. 'I've got more than enough experience to do my job, and it's not as if I'm going to be roping bulls or doing any of that kind of stuff myself!'

'True,' said Mal. 'But you do need to have some understanding of what we do, or you'll just get in the way.'

'I realise that,' she said a little stiffly. 'It's one of the reasons I'm here, after all. I want to learn as much as I can about how things work out here.'

There was a flicker of surprise in Mal's eyes. 'You may find it pretty boring,' he warned.

'I'm never bored,' said Copper firmly.

It wasn't strictly true. She was a believer in living life to the full, and crammed as much as possible into every day, but on the few occasions when she found herself with nothing to do, her zest quickly degenerated into restlessness and she would end up inventing jobs for herself.

'I hope you're right,' said Mal, but not as if he believed it very much.

'I am.' Copper decided it was time to start steering the conversation towards business. 'I'm looking forward to seeing as much of Birraminda as I can,' she said, rather pleased with her brisk tone. Now that she had got over the initial shock, it was easy to treat him as a stranger—a colleague, perhaps, or just someone to do business with.

'I'll see what we can do,' he said, but he was looking at her so strangely that Copper rubbed a surreptitious finger under her eyes in case her mascara had smudged. 'Anyway,' he went on, 'you're here now, so we'll just have to make the best of it. If you're prepared to put up with the state of things, then I'm sure we can work something out.'

It didn't sound *that* encouraging, but at least he hadn't refused to have anything to do with her, and Copper refused to be disheartened. 'That's fine by me,' she said heartily.

Mal stared at her for a moment, his expression quite impenetrable, and then all at once he seemed to relax. 'Good,' he said, and then, just when she was least expecting it, he smiled and Copper's heart flipped over.

It was only a smile, she told herself desperately, trying not to notice how the creases deepened at the corners of his mouth and eyes, how the cool, watchful look dissolved into warmth and devastating charm, how white his teeth were against his tan. Trying not to notice the way his smile reverberated the length of her spine and tingled down to her toes.

'I'm sorry I haven't been very welcoming,' he was saying. 'We've had so many girls who come for a few weeks and then rush home because they can't cope with the life out here that I've got too cynical, but if you really do want to get to know Birraminda, and aren't afraid of hard work, then we're glad to have you.' He looked across at Copper and something stirred in the depths of his eyes. 'Very glad,' he amended softly, and held out his hand.

Copper wasn't listening. She was still concentrating on breathing, in and out, very carefully. This was business, remember? she castigated herself. She would never convince Mal that she was a professional if she went to pieces every time he smiled. It was only two lips curving, a mere twitch of the facial muscles; it was absolutely stupid to let it affect her like this, especially when she had just decided to put her memories of Mal in a mental locker firmly marked 'Forgotten'. She was being worse than stupid; she was being pathetic.

Her gaze focused suddenly on Mal, who was watching her, one eyebrow lifted in faint surprise at her expression, and her heart sank as her eyes dropped belatedly to the hand stretched out to her across the table. She could hardly ignore it. Now she would have to cope with touching him as well! That was all she needed!

Bracing herself, Copper seized his hand before she had a chance to lose her nerve. This is a business contact, she chanted inwardly through gritted teeth. Business, business, business.

Mal's long brown fingers closed around hers in a firm clasp, and in spite of all her efforts to resist Copper felt her senses magically sharpen. It *was* a sort of magic, she thought incoherently. How else could she be so excruciatingly aware of everything? She could feel each line on his palm, each crease in his fingers, and his face was lit with a new clarity so that she could see every tiny detail: the thickness of his lashes, the way his hair grew, the faint scar just above his jaw. Copper could remember tracing its line with her fingers, could remember Mal telling her how it had happened, could remember exactly how it had felt to touch her lips to the warm, male-rough skin and tickle the pale line with her tongue...

CHAPTER TWO

'AHA! Holding hands already!'

So much for her senses being heightened! Copper hadn't even heard the clatter of boots on the verandah steps, and when the kitchen door burst open she jerked her hand out of Mal's as if she had been caught in the most passionate of clinches, her cheeks burning.

One of the most handsome men she had ever seen stood in the doorway. He was as tall as Mal, but much fairer, with sun-streaked hair, merry blue eyes and an air of almost tangible charm. Laughing, he tossed Megan up in his arms.

'You see what happens when you leave your father alone with a pretty girl!'

'Brett!' An expression of weary resignation and something else Copper couldn't quite identify swept across Mal's face. 'Have you finished those cattle?'

'The boys can finish them,' said Brett carelessly, apparently oblivious to Mal's frown. 'When Megan told me Dad had got a beautiful girl all to himself, I had to come and see for myself.' The dancing blue eyes studied Copper approvingly as he let his niece down, and his gaiety was so infectious that she found herself smiling back at him.

'This is my brother, Brett,' said Mal. His face was wiped of all expression, but there was a rigid set to his jaw and a muscle jumped in his cheek. 'Brett, this is Copper—' He stopped, obviously trying to remember her surname.

'Copley,' she said helpfully. 'I know it sounds silly, but there was another Caroline at school so I used to get called by my surname. Somehow Copley became Copper, and then I was stuck with it. Nobody calls me Caroline now, except my family, and I think some of my friends don't even realise that Copper's not my real name.'

'Sounds like Mal,' said Brett, ignoring Mal's warning look and pulling out the chair next to Copper's. 'He was lumbered with three names—Matthew Anthony Langland Standish—so we always shortened it to Mal when we were kids, and now only business people call him Matthew.'

'Perhaps I'd better call you Matthew, then,' said Copper, turning to Mal. It seemed like a good opportunity to establish the appropriate relations.

Mal frowned slightly. 'I hardly think that's necessary,' he said. 'If you're going to be living here as a member of the family, there's no need to be formal.'

'Absolutely not,' Brett agreed, running a lazily appreciative eye over Copper as he shook her hand with mock solemnity. 'We're going to use your nickname, so we can all be informal together. Copper suits you,' he added, reaching out a hand to touch her hair. 'Beautiful name…it sounds warm and burnished, like your hair.'

Copper's lips twitched. He was obviously a terrible flirt. She glanced at Mal from under her lashes. He was watching them with a dour expression, looking dark and stern in contrast to Brett's golden, laughing presence. It was odd that the less handsome brother should be so much more intriguing. Brett was easily the better-looking, but he lacked Mal's air of quiet, coiled strength, and when he touched her hand she felt no jolt of awareness, no tingling of the nerves, no clutch at the heart as she did just looking at Mal.

She could sense his displeasure coming in waves across the table, and it was enough to make her smile charmingly back at Brett. After all, what did she care what he thought of her? Hadn't she already decided that he meant no more than any other stranger? 'Don't tell me!' she said. 'Next you'll be saying that all I need is a good rub to make me all bright and shiny!'

Brett laughed. 'I think you're quite bright and shiny enough already,' he said.

Mal's mouth was turned down at the corner. 'I think you should go back and keep an eye on the jackaroos,' he said pointedly to his brother.

'They'll be fine.' Brett waved a dismissive hand. 'It's more important for me to be here to welcome the new housekeeper.'

'Oh?' said Copper, not sorry to divert Mal's attention in spite of her bravado. 'Are you expecting someone else today?'

There was a short silence. Mal and Brett both looked at her. 'Just you,' said Mal, but there was an ominous note in his voice.

Copper glanced from one to the other, sensing that something was wrong. 'When's the new housekeeper coming, then?'

'What new housekeeper?' said Brett in surprise. '*You're* the new housekeeper!'

She goggled at him. 'Me?'

Mal's brows had snapped together. 'Do you mean to tell us that you're *not* here to replace Kim?'

'Of course not!' said Copper indignantly. 'Do I look like a housekeeper?'

'Why do you think I was surprised to see you in a

suit?' he retorted with a trace of weariness, and pinched the bridge of his nose. 'The agency in Brisbane said they were sending a new girl out from there nearly a week ago, so I just assumed that's who you were.'

'Well, that explains why you thought I should have come on the bus, anyway,' she said.

'It doesn't explain what you're doing here, though, does it?' There was a slight edge to Mal's words and Copper found herself sitting up straighter.

'I thought you'd had my father's letter,' she said, not very clearly.

A hint of impatience was beginning to crack Mal's imperturbable mask. 'What letter?'

'The letter he wrote you a couple of weeks ago, telling you that he'd had a heart attack and that I'd be coming up in his place.' Copper looked at him expectantly, but Mal was obviously none the wiser and only holding onto his temper with difficulty. 'Dan Copley? Copley Travel?' she hurried on, hoping to jog his memory. He might not remember what had happened seven years ago, but surely he could manage a matter of weeks? 'He was here two or three months ago. He came to talk to you about the possibility of using Birraminda as a site for the new tours we're planning.'

Recognition dawned at last in Mal's eyes. 'Oh, yes, I remember,' he said. 'But what's that got to do with you turning up here?'

'I've come to negotiate a deal with you, of course,' said Copper, surprised.

'Deal?' Mal brought his hand down flat on the table and leant forward. 'What *deal*?' he asked. He didn't raise his voice but something in his expression made her lean warily back into her chair. 'I never agreed to any deal!'

'I know.' Copper stiffened her spine. She had dealt with worse people than Mal Standish. 'But you did agree to let Dad come back when he had a viable financial plan. You said you'd be prepared to discuss terms if he could convince you then that the project would work.'

Rather to her relief, he sat back and the dangerous look faded from his face. 'I might have said that,' he admitted. 'But I can't say I ever thought he would put a plan together. The whole idea seemed mad to me!'

'It's not a mad idea,' said Copper coldly. 'It's an extremely good idea. Lots of people would like to experience the outback in style. They don't want to sit on buses or stay in hotels, but they don't necessarily want to crawl around in a tiny tent either. We're going to offer permanent safari tents with camp beds and a bathroom, as well as fine cooking and specialist leaders for the different groups—expert artists, ornithologists, people like that,' she finished, with an airy wave of the hand.

'It sounds good to me,' enthused Brett. 'Especially if they're prepared to pay pots of money for the privilege of getting squawked at by treefuls of cockatoos!'

'Well, money is certainly something we'd have to discuss,' said Copper carefully.

'Right now we're not going to discuss anything,' said Mal with an air of flat finality. 'I'm sorry that your father's been ill, but, frankly, you couldn't have picked a worse time. If I'd realised you were coming, I could have told you not to bother.'

'But my father wrote to you,' she protested. 'That's why I thought you were expecting me. You must have had the letter!'

'I may have.' He shrugged his indifference. 'There's been so much to do here recently, and things have been so chaotic since Kim left that any paperwork that's not absolutely urgent has just had to wait.'

Copper eyed him with growing resentment. It might not have been urgent to him, but if he'd bothered to read the letter he could have saved her a three-day drive from Adelaide!

'I'm here now,' she pointed out. 'Couldn't you at least listen to our proposals?'

'No,' said Mal flatly. 'I've got too many other things on my mind at the moment, especially since you're not anything useful like a housekeeper. I need one of those more than I need a crackpot scheme that sounds like nothing but trouble from start to finish. I've got no one to look after the house, I've got no one to look after my daughter and I've got no rain.' Picking up his hat, he got to his feet. 'What I *have* got is eighty thousand head of cattle, and a thousand of them are out there in the holding yards right now, so you'll have to excuse us.' He jerked his head towards the door. 'That "us" includes you, Brett. We've still got work to do.'

Settling his hat on his head, Mal looked down at Copper. Her chin was set at a stubborn angle and the green eyes were mutinous. She was still seething over the way he had dismissed their cherished project. Her father had invested everything in the success of these tours. The whole future of Copley Travel was at stake and all Mal could say was that it sounded a crackpot scheme!

'You can stay tonight, of course,' he said to her. 'But I can tell you now that we won't be doing any discussing.'

Behind Mal's back, Brett gave Copper a sympathetic grin. 'I'm sure we'll be able to find something else to do,' he said meaningfully, and winked at her.

Mal's mouth tightened. 'Come on, Brett,' he snapped. 'We've wasted enough time today as it is.'

Charming! Copper glared after them. All those years of dreaming about Mal and what it would be like to meet him again, and all she turned out to be was a waste of his time!

In a way she was glad that he had been so objectionable. It made it much easier to ignore the way her heart had leapt at the sight of him, the treacherous way her body had responded to one brief smile. Now she really could put the past behind her.

Copper's eyes narrowed as she remembered how Mal had refused even to listen to her proposals. She had driven a file full of proposals all the way from Adelaide, and if he thought she was going to meekly turn around and go home tomorrow, he was very much mistaken!

Worry over the future of Copley Travel had almost killed her father, and the prospect of restoring their fortunes by investing in a project that would appeal to the quality end of the market was all that was keeping him going. The company had been Dan Copley's life, and the luxury outback tours a long-held dream. While he had been in hospital, Copper had taken over the project, working all hours of the day and night to get to the stage where they could confidently approach Matthew Standish again. And Mal had refused to listen just because he didn't have anyone to wash up for him!

Well, he would soon learn that Copper had no intention of taking no for an answer! If politely asking wouldn't make Mal listen, then she would have to find some other way of convincing him that she meant business!

When Mal came back, much later, Copper was sitting on the verandah outside the kitchen door, looking out over the creek. Megan sat beside her in a clean nightie, chattering about life on the station. Her face sparkled and her dusky curls had been brushed until they shone. 'There's Dad!' she interrupted herself suddenly, pointing, and Copper's heart promptly jumped to her throat, where it lodged, fluttering wildly in spite of all her stern attempts to subdue it.

Grateful for the fading light, she watched Mal walking towards them through the dusk. There was a lithe, unconscious grace about the way he moved, an ease and assurance in his stride that stirred something in the pit of Copper's stomach. Megan was dancing barefoot at the top of the steps.

'Dad, Dad, we've got a surprise for you!'

Copper forced herself not to notice as Mal smiled down at his daughter and lifted her up into his arms.

'You've had a bath,' he said as Megan hugged her arms around his neck.

'Copper bathed me, and she sang a funny song.'

'Did she now?' Shifting Megan onto his hip, Mal looked over to where Copper sat in a low wicker chair. She had showered and changed into a sleeveless white shirt and narrow trousers. Her shiny brown hair was still wet, and her tilted lashes clung damply together, but she hoped she looked cool and comfortable and suitably dressed at last.

Tilting her chin in unconscious challenge, she looked back at him. 'You don't mind, do you?'

'Of course not.' There was an odd note in his voice, but before Copper could speculate as to what it might mean Megan was wriggling to be let down.

'Can I show you the surprise now?'

'I thought the surprise was you being bathed and

ready for bed?' he teased, but Megan shook her head solemnly.

'No, this is a proper surprise.'

Mal lifted his brows in silent enquiry at Copper, but she just smiled blandly. She was saving the real surprise until later.

Megan dragged her father into the kitchen. Through the screen, Copper could hear the counterpoint between the two voices, one high and excited, the other calm and deep, and she smiled to herself as she listened, content for once to sit quietly and watch the sunset. It had been a long day and tiredness was buzzing along her bones.

It was some time before Mal reappeared, carrying two bottles of beer. He handed one to Copper and the wicker creaked as he sat down on the chair next to hers. The beer was so cold that condensation ran down the outside and Copper had to keep shifting it from hand to hand.

'Where's Megan?' she asked.

'In bed.'

'And Brett?'

'Having a shower.' Mal had showered too. His hair was damp and she could smell the soap on his clean skin as he leant forward, resting his arms on his knees, and turning the beer bottle thoughtfully between his hands.

Copper found herself watching them as if mesmerised. She had loved Mal's hands. They were strong and brown, with long, deft fingers that had traced slow patterns of fire over her skin. They had curved around her breast and smoothed the long length of her thigh, possessing her with a sureness and a hunger that had left her gasping his name.

Wrenching her eyes away, Copper took a desperate pull of beer and forced the memories back into that box labelled 'Forgotten'. She was not going to think about his hands or his mouth or anything about him at all. She was going to think business.

It had grown dark while Mal had been inside, and the only light came from the blue lamp that was set below the verandah to attract flying insects. At regular intervals it would fizz and crackle as one got too close and was zapped out of existence. Copper watched it in silence and tried to think how to bring the conversation round to her new proposal.

In the end it was Mal who spoke first. 'You've been busy,' he said. 'It must have taken you a long time to clean that kitchen.'

Copper shrugged. 'Megan helped me.' In fact, Megan had been more of a hindrance than a help, but she had been so thrilled to be in on the surprise that Copper hadn't had the heart to discourage her. Together they had tidied the clutter off the table and washed the huge pile of dishes. Then they had swept the floor and wiped the surfaces until everything gleamed. There had been no time to clean the fridge or sort out the cupboards, but Copper felt that the contrast with the earlier mess would be enough to make an impact.

Mal was still turning the bottle slowly between his hands. 'I don't want you to think I don't appreciate it,' he said, 'but a clean kitchen isn't enough to make me change my mind.'

'I'm not asking you to,' said Copper, and his gaze narrowed as he looked at her.

'You're not expecting me to believe that you did all that out of the goodness of your heart? You must want something!'

'I do,' she said evenly. 'I want you to give me a job.'

Mal's fingers stilled abruptly and he sat up in surprise. 'What kind of job?'

'You need a housekeeper, don't you? I'm suggesting that you let me take over until this girl from the agency turns up.'

Copper was pleased with how cool and business-like she sounded, but Mal didn't seem particularly impressed. 'What do you know about being a housekeeper?' he asked suspiciously.

He could have sounded a bit more grateful! 'What is there to know?' said Copper. 'You don't need any qualifications to clean a house—or do you only take girls with higher degrees in vacuuming and washing dishes?'

Mal ignored her sarcasm. 'Perhaps I should have asked why you suddenly want to be a housekeeper,' he said. 'You looked pretty offended at being mistaken for one earlier on.'

'I don't want to be a housekeeper,' she said, 'but I do want to stay at Birraminda. And if it means spending a few days working as hard as I did this afternoon, then I'm prepared to do that.'

'And in return I have to agree to let you and your father set up this mad scheme of yours?' Mal set his beer on the floor and shook his head. 'I can't deny I need a housekeeper, but I don't want one badly enough to commit Birraminda to an enterprise that could involve us in a lot of disruption and hassle. Even if it's a wild success, the financial return isn't likely to be enough to make it worth our while.'

Copper took a steadying breath. This was not the time to prove to Mal that he had quite the wrong idea about the project. 'I'm not asking you to agree,' she said. 'At least, not yet. All I'm asking is for you to put aside some time to just listen to our proposals before I leave. I'm sure that if I showed you our plans I'd be able to convince you that they could be good for you as well as for us, but I'd rather wait until you can give them your full attention. In the meantime, I'll keep house for you.'

She glanced at him, wishing that she could read the expression on his face. 'It's a good offer,' she assured him. 'An hour of your time in return for free house-keeping.'

'You mean you wouldn't expect any payment?' Mal raised his brows in disbelief.

'All I'd ask is a chance to see a bit more of Birraminda. There are still a lot of practical details we have to sort out and I really need to see the sites my father chose for myself.'

There was a pause. Mal picked up his beer again and took a pull, his eyes on the crackling blue light. 'This eagerness to stay wouldn't be anything to do with my brother, would it?' he asked at last.

'With Brett?' Copper stared at him. 'What would it have to do with him?'

Mal shrugged. 'He can be very charming.'

'I realise that, but if you think I'd be prepared to spend my days cooking and cleaning just to be near him, you must be out of your mind!'

'You wouldn't say that if you'd seen as many girls make fools of themselves over him as I have.' Mal rubbed a weary hand over his face. 'Brett, as you've probably gathered, is physically incapable of being in the same room as a woman without flirting with her. He doesn't take it seriously—Brett doesn't take anything se-riously—but the agency keeps sending us girls who think they're the only one he's ever kissed. They fall madly in love with him, he gets bored after a week or so, and it all ends in tears. The next thing I know, they're on the bus back to Brisbane. Once the passionate affair is over, there isn't any way of avoiding each other out here,' he added in a dry voice.

Was that some kind of hint? Copper looked at him sharply. She had the best of reasons for knowing that it was true, but did Mal realise? Not for the first time, she cursed the impossibility of ever knowing just what he was thinking.

'I can imagine it's rather difficult,' she said after a moment. Her voice held a slight chill. If Mal remembered their own passionate affair, he could come right out and say so. *She* certainly wasn't going to mention it! 'Why don't you ask the agency to send an older woman?'

'Do you think I haven't thought of that?' Mal sighed. 'It isn't that easy. There aren't many middle-aged women who are prepared to give up comfortable lives to come and live somewhere like this. It's not exactly a career opportunity. Even the younger girls will only come out on short contracts. There isn't anything for them to do and they get bored, so none of them are going to stay permanently, but they might stay a bit longer if it wasn't for Brett.'

'Can't you ask him to leave them alone?'

Mal smiled but there was no humour in it. 'Sure— and I could ask him to stop breathing while I'm at it!'

'It must make it very difficult for Megan with all these girls coming and going,' said Copper, and he frowned.

'I know, but what can I do?'

'If Brett won't stop flirting, you could always tell him to leave,' she suggested.

'And go where?' Mal got irritably to his feet and walked over to lean against the rail. 'Brett grew up at Birraminda and it's part of his inheritance. Oh, I know he can be absolutely infuriating at times, but I can't just turn him off. He's my brother.'

'Doesn't he realise how difficult he's making things for you?' asked Copper curiously.

At the rail, Mal shrugged. 'He's always sorry when I explain why yet another housekeeper has left, but you've seen what he's like. Criticism just runs off his back, and somehow it's impossible to stay cross with him for very long. He's nearly ten years younger than me, so he was always the baby of the family. That's probably why he's never learnt any responsibility.'

Turning round to face Copper once more, he leant back against the rail and crossed his ankles. 'It doesn't help that I run things here at Birraminda. Brett would soon learn responsibility if he had his own property to run, but property doesn't come cheap, and we've been working flat out to make enough to invest in more land. That's one of the reasons I was prepared to listen to your father when he was here. I'd hoped that there might be some money for us in his project, but once I heard what he was planning I soon gave that idea up!'

'Well, maybe I'll be able to change your mind about that,' said Copper with a tight smile. 'I won't try and persuade you now, though. I'll wait until you let me have that hour—if you accept my offer, of course.' She lifted her chin at him. 'I think I can safely promise you that I won't fall in love with Brett!'

'You seem very sure of that,' said Mal, eyeing her speculatively.

'I am. I like your brother very much, but he's really not my type. Besides,' she hurried on, before Mal decided to ask her just what her type *was*, 'I happen to already be in love with someone else.'

Mal didn't move, and his expression didn't change,

but Copper had the feeling that the air had tightened somehow. 'Someone in Adelaide?' he said, without any inflection in his voice at all.

'Yes.' Mentally she crossed her fingers, thinking of Glyn who had been her boyfriend until a month ago. They had had some good times together, and in spite of the way it had ended Copper knew that she would always be fond of him. She wasn't in love with him now, but there was no need to tell Mal that. All Mal needed to know was that she was serious about staying at Birraminda until she had had a chance to convince him that Copley Travel meant business.

'I see,' said Mal.

'So, do we have a deal?' she asked with forced brightness.

'It'll be hard work,' he warned. 'This won't be like working in an office. You and your father seem to have some romantic ideas about the outback, but it's a tough life. The days are long and hot and dusty, and at the end of them there's nowhere to go and no one else to see. You'll have the most boring jobs to do and no one to help you. It won't be at all romantic.'

'I'm not in the slightest bit romantic,' said Copper icily.

It was true. Copper liked life as it was, and didn't believe in dreaming about the way things might be. Her friends would fall about with laughter if they knew she had been accused of being romantic, but then, she hadn't told any of them about the three days she had spent with Mal in Turkey. That had been stepping out of time and out of character. For Copper, it had been too special to share with anyone else. Mal had been her secret, her aberration, her one brief encounter with romance.

'That must be very disappointing for your boyfriend,' said Mal, with something of a sneer.

Looking back, Copper thought that it probably *had* been disappointing for Glyn, but she had no intention of admitting as much to Mal.

'It depends what you mean by romantic, doesn't it?' she challenged him. 'I prefer to get on with things rather than mope around wishing they were different.'

Oh, yes? said an inner voice. So why did you never quite manage to forget about Mal, no matter how hard you tried? Why were you so hurt when he didn't remember you?

'Anyway,' Copper went on, firmly squashing the voice, 'all you need to know is that I'll work hard and I won't waste my time dreaming about your brother. As far as I'm concerned Birraminda is business, and I'm not interested in anything else up here.'

Mal studied her in silence for a moment. Copper would have given anything to know what he was thinking, but as usual he kept his reactions to himself. 'OK,' he said at last, straightening from the rail. 'You can stay on as housekeeper—but only until the girl from the agency turns up. She should be here any day.'

'That's all right,' said Copper, getting to her feet in relief at having passed the first hurdle. At least she wouldn't have to drive back to Adelaide tomorrow! 'And you will give me an opportunity to show you our proposal?'

'As long as you don't mention it the rest of the time,' said Mal stringently. 'I don't want you nagging at me. You can bring out your financial plan and your proposals, but you're only getting one chance to talk me round.'

Copper smiled. 'One will be enough,' she said.

CHAPTER THREE

BY LUNCHTIME the next day, Copper was exhausted. Mal hadn't been wrong about the hard work. She had been up at five to cook breakfast for Mal and Brett, as well as the three jackaroos, and she seemed to have spent the whole morning since then running between the cookhouse and the homestead.

She had washed and wiped, swept and scrubbed. She had fed chickens and dogs and six men who had appeared for morning smoko and now lunch, and in the middle of it all she had had to deal with a lively and strong-willed four-year-old.

It hadn't helped that she had spent most of the night lying awake and thinking about Mal—the one thing she had sworn not to do. Her body had craved sleep, but her mind had refused to settle. It had turned Mal's image round and round, testing it from all angles, disconcerted to find him at once so familiar and yet a stranger. Did he really not remember? Had he forgotten touching her, tasting her with his tongue, tangling his fingers in her hair as they surrendered to the wild beat of their bodies?

Copper had struggled to bury the memories. She was at Birraminda on business, she'd told herself fiercely, gritting her teeth as she worked doggedly through the morning. It was the business that mattered now, and she had better not forget it.

She had had lunch with the jackaroos and all the other men except Bill in the cookhouse. It was a long, wooden building that didn't look as if it had been decorated since the days when sixty thousand sheep had grazed at Birraminda and whole teams of men had moved in at shearing time and had to be fed at the two huge tables. Bill was an older man who was known as the "married man". While the jackaroos slept in quarters he had his own house a mile or so from the homestead, and he went home at lunchtime. His wife, Naomi, prepared a meal for the men in the evenings, so that was one job she wouldn't have to do, Copper thought. Dinner for three ought to be a cinch after all she had done this morning!

Mal had told her that cold meat and bread were all that the men wanted at lunchtime, so that had not been too difficult to get ready. Now Copper ticked 'lunch' off her list and studied her remaining chores, wondering if she would have time to explore around the homestead. She would need to take photographs and get the feel of the place if she was to put together an inspiring brochure.

'What are you doing?' asked Mal, craning his head to see as she pencilled times against 'prepare vegetables' and 'bath Megan'. He raised his eyebrows derisively when he saw what she had written. 'I never met anyone who had to have a timetable just to get through the day before!'

'I like to be organised,' said Copper, instantly on the defensive. 'Otherwise nothing ever gets done.'

'I hope you've given yourself time for breathing.' Mal wasn't actually smiling but she knew perfectly well that he was laughing at her.

'I need to with this much to do!' she retorted, more ruffled than she cared to admit by the amusement gleaming in the depths of his brown eyes. 'I hadn't realised slavery was still legal in the outback!'

Brett twitched the list out of her hand. 'You've been

working much too hard,' he agreed. He had greeted the news that Copper was to stay with flattering enthusiasm, and now he edged along the bench towards her. 'You deserve a break this afternoon,' he went on, echoing Copper's own thoughts. 'Why don't I take you out and show you the waterhole your father had in mind for a site?'

'Possibly because you've remembered that you're going to check those bores this afternoon,' Mal interrupted, before Copper had a chance to accept. His voice was quiet but implacable. 'Megan and I will take Copper out.'

Megan looked up, suddenly alert. 'Are we going to ride?'

Mal glanced at Copper. She was more practically dressed today, in jeans and a fresh, mint-coloured shirt, but there was still something indefinably citified about her. Over lunch, all the talk had been about the forthcoming rodeo, and the expressive green eyes had been appalled at the thought of wrestling a steer to the ground, or trying to cling onto a bucking bronco.

'I think Copper would probably prefer to go in the car,' he said, but a smile lurked around his mouth.

Copper stiffened, well aware of how out of place she looked. 'Not at all,' she said, lifting her chin. She wasn't going to give Mal the excuse of dismissing her proposals just because he thought she couldn't cope in the outback! So what if she had never ridden before? It couldn't be that difficult. 'I'd like to ride.'

She regretted her bravado as soon as she laid eyes on the horse that Mal led towards her. It looked enormous, and as Copper edged closer it rolled its eyes and shook the flies off its mane with a snort. Backing rapidly away, she clutched her wallet file nervously to her chest. Maybe the car would be a better idea.

Mal nodded at the file. 'What have you got there?'

'Just a few things I want to check—Dad's plan of the site, the measurements of the tent, that kind of thing—and I'm bound to need to take some notes.'

'Where are you going to put it?' he asked in exasperation. 'Or were you planning to ride one-handed?'

Copper hadn't even thought about it until that moment. 'Isn't there a saddle-bag or something?'

Mal sighed. 'Here, give it to me. I'll hold it while you get on.'

'Right.' She blew out a breath and squared her shoulders. 'Right.'

The horse tossed its head up and down impatiently as Copper seized the reins. She had seen this lots of times on television. All she had to do was put one foot in the stirrup and throw her other leg over. There was nothing to it.

On television, though, the horses stood obligingly still. *This* horse danced sideways as soon as she got her foot into the stirrup, and she ended up hopping around the yard while the three jackaroos sitting on the fence watched with broad grins. Tipping their hats back, they had the air of settling down for a rare afternoon's entertainment.

Cursing the horse under her breath, Copper clenched her teeth and hopped harder. Mal shook his head with a mixture of amusement and exasperation. 'Would it help if I held him?' he asked, the very politeness of his voice a humiliation. He took hold of the bridle, and the horse, sensing the hand of a master, stopped dead.

'Thank you,' said Copper grittily. Gathering the reins more firmly in her hand, she tried again, but with no more success than before, and in the end Mal had to take her foot and boost her unceremoniously up into the saddle where she landed with a bump.

'Oh, my God,' she muttered, horrified to find herself so far from the ground. She would need a parachute to get down again! Too nervous to notice the resigned expression on Mal's face, she stared straight ahead as he let the horse go and stepped back.

Flicking its ears at the delay, the horse immediately set off. 'Whoa!' squawked Copper in alarm, and yanked at the reins, but it only seemed to take that as encouragement and broke into a brisk trot around the yard. Copper's feet bumped out of the stirrups and she bounced hopelessly around in the saddle, bawling at the horse to stop. Somewhere in the background, she could hear the sound of heartless laughter. At least someone was enjoying themselves!

The horse was heading straight for the gate into the paddock. Oh, God, what if it decided to jump? 'Who-oo-oo-oa!' yelled Copper, pulling frantically at the reins, and the horse turned smartly, sending her lurching sideways before it discovered Mal barring its way and stopped dead. Unprepared, Copper pitched forward, slithered down its neck and landed on her bottom in an undignified heap at Mal's feet.

He was grinning callously. 'Are you OK?' he asked, not even bothering to conceal his amusement as Megan squealed with laughter and the jackaroos hooted and whistled from the fence.

Without waiting for an answer, Mal reached down and put a firm hand beneath her arm to lift her easily to her feet. Copper was very conscious of the strength in his fingers and the whiteness of his teeth against his brown skin as he grinned. She jerked her arm away and made a great show of brushing the dust off the seat of her jeans. 'I think so,' she said a little sulkily. Much he would have cared if she had broken her leg! That would have been *really* funny, wouldn't it?

'Why didn't you tell me you couldn't ride?' Mal asked, his voice still warm with amusement.

'I didn't think you'd put me on a beastly wild horse!' snapped Copper, almost disappointed to discover that the only injury was to her pride. It would have served him right if she had had to be stretchered back to Adelaide!

Mal only laughed. 'Wild? Old Duke here is the laziest horse we've got. I picked him specially for you.'

'Sweet of you,' she said between her teeth. 'Remind me never to ask you for anything else special!'

'How did you think you were going to manage with a file under your arm when you'd never ridden before?' He shook his head. 'Wish I'd seen it, though! It would have made quite a story to keep us going in the wet!'

'Perhaps I'll just take a notebook,' said Copper coldly. 'I can put it in my shirt pocket—or is that too bizarre for you?'

'You want to have another go?'

Copper looked over at the grinning jackaroos. The youngest cupped his hands around his mouth. 'Hey, Copper!' he shouted. 'We're going to enter you for the bucking bronco at the rodeo! Better get in some more practice!'

'Why not?' she said. 'I'd hate to deprive you all of such good entertainment!'

'Good girl.' Mal smiled at her and turned to send one of the boys for a leading rein. 'We'll keep good hold of you this time,' he said, and gave her a leg up back into the saddle. 'Look, you hold the reins like this.' He looked up at her and her heart seemed to stop. She saw his face in sudden and startling detail: the grooves at either side of his mouth, the smile crinkling his eyes, the prickle of stubble along his jaw. 'Relax!' he said, giving the strap a final tug to secure it and slapping Duke's rump affectionately.

Copper smiled weakly and managed to look away. 'I think I've got altitude sickness!' she said. That would account for the queer feeling in the pit of her stomach, anyway.

Mal rolled his eyes, but his smile burned behind her eyelids as he swung himself easily onto an enormous chestnut horse with a star on its forehead. The jackaroo attached a leading rein to Duke's bridle and handed the end up to Mal, who moved his horse up beside her. 'Ready?'

'Yes.' Copper cleared her throat. 'Yes,' she said again, more firmly this time.

Megan was already on her pony, trotting it around in circles with humiliating ease. The gate was swung open. Mal touched his heels to his horse's flanks, clicked his tongue behind his teeth to urge Duke forward, and Copper found herself riding.

They took it very slowly at first. Megan trotted ahead on her pony, but the two horses ambled contentedly together. The lack of speed didn't seem to bother Mal, but then it wouldn't, Copper thought. He was never hurried, never flustered, never nervous. She was very conscious of him sitting relaxed in the saddle, his eyes creased as he scanned the horizon instinctively and his outline uncannily distinct in the fierce outback light.

Copper felt very safe knowing that he could control her horse as well as his own, and after a while she, too, began to relax and look around her. They were following the line of the creek, picking their way through the spin-

dly gums that spread out from the watercourse. It was
very quiet. In the heat of the afternoon the birds were
mostly silent, and there was just the creak of the saddles
and the rustle of leaves beneath the horses' hooves as
they kicked up a distinctive dry fragrance. Copper
breathed it in as it mingled with the smell of leather in
her hands.

She was very aware of Mal, overwhelmingly solid beside her. Unlike her, he wore no sunglasses, but the brim
of his hat threw a shadow that divided his face in two.
Above, his eyes were hidden, but below, his mouth was
very clear, cool and firm and peculiarly exciting.

It was just a mouth, just two lips. Copper stared desperately ahead between Duke's ears, but it tugged
irresistibly at the corner of her vision and her eyes kept
skittering sideways in spite of herself. Every time they
rested on his mouth, the breath would dry in her throat
and she would look quickly away.

She was so taken up with keeping her eyes under control that she didn't notice at first that Mal had brought
the horses to a halt in a clearing beside the creek. He
swung himself off his horse and looped its reins around
the branch of a fallen tree before lifting Megan off her
pony. She ran happily down to the water's edge, where
there was a tiny sandy beach, and Mal turned to Copper,
who was wondering how she was going to get off. Perhaps she should just try falling off like before?

'Take your foot out of the stirrup,' he said. 'Then
swing your leg over the saddle. I'll catch you.'

He held his arms up as he spoke but a paralysing
shyness had Copper in its grip once more and she could
only stare helplessly down at him and wish that he had
never been married, that the last seven years would sim-

ply dissolve and leave them as they had been then, a man and a girl bound briefly by magic.

'Come on,' said Mal as she hesitated still. 'You're going to have to get off some time!'

Somehow Copper managed to wriggle one leg over the saddle, and the next thing she knew she was slithering clumsily to the ground, Mal's hands hard at her waist. He held her for a moment and she stood with her hands resting on his shoulders for support, struggling against the overwhelming temptation to slide them round his neck and lean against him.

'Thank you,' she muttered, unable to meet his eyes in case he read the longing in her own, and after a tiny moment he let her go.

'This is where your father wanted to put the camp,' said Mal, looking around him at the tranquil scene.

'It looks perfect.' Copper cleared her throat and moved away from him in what she hoped would look a casual way. 'Well, I...I'd better take some notes.'

She threw herself into looking busy. She paced out the site and stopped to make notes, but her mind wasn't on siting tents or camp kitchens. It was on Mal, leading the horses down to the creek to drink before he tethered them in the shade. He looked tough and self-contained and somehow *right*, she thought, watching him move through the splintered light beneath the trees with his deliberate, unhurried tread. There was something uncompromising about him that belonged with this unrelenting landscape.

Then Mal turned to see her watching him, and Copper hurriedly bent her head back over her notebook. She couldn't take notes for ever, though, and when she thought she had impressed him enough with the fact that she only cared about business, she went to join him on the fallen tree.

Mal moved along to make room for her. There was an ironic look about his mouth as she put her notebook away. He made no comment but Copper had the feeling that he knew perfectly well that all her rushing around had just been for show, and she avoided his eye as she sat down beside him.

For a while they sat without speaking, watching Megan who was busily scooping water from the creek for some unseen project that seemed to involve a good deal of mess and mud. Behind them, the horses shifted their legs and blew softly. Slowly the peace settled around Copper, and some of the tension went out of her shoulders.

'It's a beautiful place,' she said at last.

'Yes.' Mal looked around him, and then at her. 'It wouldn't be so beautiful with a clutter of tents and a busload of tourists, though, would it?'

Copper met his eyes squarely, her own green and direct. 'Everything would be in keeping with the landscape,' she said. 'I think you'd be surprised at how beautiful it will all still be, but I'm not going to try and convince you now.' She smiled. 'I haven't forgotten what we agreed and I'm not going to waste my one chance!'

'Oh, yes, talking of our agreement...' Mal tipped his hat and resettled it on his head. 'I rang the agency at lunchtime to find out what had happened to my new housekeeper. Apparently she got offered a job as a waitress in town at the last minute and decided to take that instead.'

Copper looked at the trees reflected in the glassy water and wondered why anyone would choose to work in a restaurant when they could be somewhere like this. Then she thought about the chores she had slogged through that morning and decided that the girl, whoever she was, might have made a sensible decision.

'Are they going to send someone else?'

'They haven't got anyone immediately available, so they're going to have to advertise. It'll be at least a week before I get someone else, maybe longer.' Mal glanced at her. 'Think you can stand it for that long?'

'Of course,' said Copper, secretly relieved. She wasn't ready to go back to Adelaide yet, but nor was she ready to enquire too closely into the reasons for her reluctance to leave Birraminda. 'I said I'd stay until you got a proper housekeeper, and I will.'

'What about your commitments at home?'

'That's not a problem,' she said with some surprise. 'We got someone in to help out at the office so that I could concentrate on our plans for here, and Dad can keep an eye on things. It's not a very busy time of year, anyway.'

'I was thinking more of personal commitments,' said Mal dryly. 'Isn't anyone going to miss you?'

Would anyone miss her? She had plenty of friends who would wonder aloud where she was and wish that she was around to get a party going, but they were as busy as she was and their lives wouldn't stop without her.

'No,' said Copper with a sad smile. 'I don't think anyone will miss me very much.'

'What about this man you're so in love with?'

She had forgotten that she had told him about Glyn. 'I don't think he'll notice much difference.' She sighed and stirred some curls of dried bark in the dust with her foot. 'He was always complaining that I was never at home, anyway. I have to travel a lot, and when I'm in Adelaide there's so much paperwork to catch up with at the office. I can't be home at four o'clock every day, just waiting for him to come home.'

'You could get a different job,' said Mal.

'You sound like Glyn,' she said bitterly. 'Quite apart from the fact that Dad needs me now, I love my job. Why should I give it up?'

'No reason, if your job is more important to you than your boyfriend.'

'Why does it always have to be a choice between them?' Copper burst out in remembered frustration. 'I was perfectly happy with the way things were. Glyn knew what I was like. Why did I have to be the one to make all the compromises?'

'It doesn't sound as if you were prepared to make any compromises,' commented Mal, with an unexpectedly harsh note in his voice, and Copper's angry resentment collapsed abruptly.

'That's what Glyn said.' She took off her hat and combed her fingers dispiritedly through her hair. 'Anyway, it doesn't matter any more. I'd been in Singapore for ten days, and when I got back Glyn said he wanted to talk to me. I made a joke about it at first, said I'd have to consult my diary to see if I could arrange an appointment, but he was dead serious. He said he was fed up with coming home to an empty house and that he didn't feel there was any point in us pretending to be a couple any longer when he spent most of his time on his own. And then he said that he'd been seeing a lot of Ellie, who's a good friend of mine. Her husband left her earlier this year, and they were both lonely, and...'

Copper tried to shrug carelessly but the memory still hurt. 'Well, in the end he said he was going to move in with her. It was all very amicable. Glyn has always been one of my friends and so has Ellie. We're all part of the same crowd. I couldn't avoid seeing either of them if I wanted to keep my friends, so we were very civilised and talked it through together.'

'And you had your job to comfort you,' Mal reminded her ironically.

'Yes, I had my job,' she said in a flat voice. What had she expected? That he would be sympathetic?

Mal leant forward, linking his fingers loosely between his knees. 'So when you said you were in love with this Glyn yesterday, you weren't telling the truth?'

'Oh, I don't know…' Copper turned her hat listlessly between her hands. 'I do love Glyn. He's a great person. We even talked about getting married once, but we never got round to it. *I* never got round to it,' she corrected herself. 'There was always too much else to do. And now I think it was all for the best. Copley Travel is too important to me to give up, and if it's meant giving up Glyn instead, well, I think he probably didn't really love me either, if he wanted me to change that much.'

Mal said nothing. It was impossible to tell whether his silence was sympathetic or contemptuous. 'Anyway,' she went on brightly after a while, 'at least you know now why I'm not in any hurry to go back to Adelaide. I really don't mind seeing Glyn and Ellie together, but it seems to make everybody else feel awkward when we're all together. If I'm away for a while, it'll give everyone a chance to get used to the situation.'

'It sounds to me as if this Glyn had a lucky escape.' Mal was watching his daughter playing happily in the sand, but his mouth was twisted as if with bitter remembrance. 'It must have been a shock for him to realise that you were prepared to put your business before everything else.

'My wife was like you,' he went on after a moment. 'She thought she could have everything. When I met her, she had her own chain of shops in Brisbane. I never thought she'd be prepared to give it all up to live out here, but Lisa liked the idea of being mistress of a huge outback station. She always thought big, and Birraminda was that all right. Of course, I made sure that she spent some time out here before we were married, so that she could see exactly what was involved, but no! Lisa knew what she wanted—and what Lisa wanted, Lisa got.'

'Why did you marry her if she was like that?' asked Copper, more sharply than she had intended. She had been prepared to be jealous of Mal's dead wife, but she hadn't expected to resent being compared to her!

'I didn't realise what she was like until it was too late,' he said. 'And she was very beautiful...' He trailed off, as if conjuring up an image. 'You'd have to have known her to understand what she was like,' he went on finally. 'She could charm the birds off the trees when she wanted to, but she had a will of iron and she never had any doubt where her priorities lay. At first she thought she could run her business from out here, so I paid a fortune to equip a special office for her.

'You should go in there some time,' he added, with a glance at Copper. 'It's got telephones, a computer, a fax machine, a photocopier—everything you need to run a business. But it wasn't enough for Lisa. She wasn't interested in cooking or cleaning, although I had a whole new kitchen put in for her as well, to help her adjust, and she was easily bored if she didn't have anything she wanted to do, so she was always nagging at me to fly her to Brisbane so that she could check up on the accounts or visit designers or negotiate some special deal or other. Oh, she was an astute businesswoman, all right.'

Why did he have to make it sound like an insult? wondered Copper, who was recognising more of herself in Lisa than she really wanted to. What was wrong with being energetic and intelligent?

'If she was that astute, she wouldn't have married you unless she really wanted to be with you,' she said after a moment.

Mal shook his head. 'That was what I thought. Of course, I had what you would call a stupidly romantic idea about marriage, but Lisa's attitude was much more practical. Marriage to me gave her a sort of position, an image of someone equally at home in the outback as in the city, but she never really liked it out here and she ended up spending more and more time back in Brisbane.'

'But what about Megan?'

'Megan was the result of a doomed attempt to save a doomed marriage,' said Mal stonily. 'It didn't work, of course. Lisa saw pregnancy as an excuse to escape permanently to the city. She said that she needed to be near a hospital, that Birraminda was no place for a baby, so she went to Brisbane and she never came back. She didn't even ring me until after the baby was born.' His mouth set in a bitter line. 'She told me her labour came on unexpectedly and that there hadn't been time to call me and tell me to come to the hospital, but it wasn't true. I was supposed to be grateful that she even let me see my own child.'

His voice was very controlled but Copper could see the rigidity in his jaw. She understood now what had put that shuttered look in his eyes and carved sternness into his face. No wonder Mal had changed. The birth of his daughter ought to have been a joyful occasion, but instead he had been excluded, rejected, denied the emotional intensity of seeing his child come into the world.

Copper wished she knew how to offer him sympathy. If she had been another girl she might have been able to take his hand, or put her arms around him, but she wasn't another girl. She had condemned herself as a girl who put her job first, just like his wife, and she was afraid that Mal would flinch from her touch.

So she only clenched her hands around the rim of her hat and said nothing.

After a while Mal went on, as if the words were being forced out of him but he needed to finish the story. 'We both knew that there was no point in pretending that the marriage was going to work after that,' he said. 'It was a relief in a way, but the divorce settlement crippled me financially. All my money's in land, and I'm still struggling to get back to the way things were before. The worst thing was leaving Megan behind, but everyone said she needed to be with her mother.'

His expression was closed, refusing pity. 'I believed it myself until I saw how she was handed over to a succession of nannies while Lisa went back to working fifteen-hour days in her business. I flew down to see her as often as I could, but the child had no chance to get to know me. When Lisa was killed in a car accident and I went to bring Megan home, she was terrified. She was only two and it must have seemed as if she was being handed over to a complete stranger.'

Copper's eyes rested on Megan, squatting by the water. Her hands were full of mud, her face grubby and absorbed, and she was chattering away to herself, oblivious to the two adults watching her. 'She seems happy enough now.'

'I think so too, when I see her like this, but she's too used to playing on her own.' Mal sighed. 'She doesn't remember much about Lisa, but she misses having a mother. It might be different if I could get a housekeeper to come out here and stay for a year or so, but these girls who come and go are just unsettling for her. She needs some security.'

'You're her security,' said Copper gently, but he shook his head.

'I'm not enough,' he said. 'I can't be around the homestead the whole time. Megan needs more attention than I can give her. Too often she has to sit on a fence where I can see her and keep out of the way. She's learning plenty about how to run a cattle station but she isn't learning enough about being a child.'

Mal's eyes rested on the curve of his daughter's back. 'Of course, what I really need is a new wife,' he said with a mirthless smile. 'But I don't think I can go through another marriage like that again.'

Copper hesitated. 'It doesn't need to be like that,' she said quietly. You didn't need to be a romantic to believe that marriage didn't have to be a battleground of conflicting interests, as Mal's had been.

'Doesn't it?' said Mal. 'Where am I going to find a woman who'd be prepared to give up everything and come and live out here? No friends, no shops, no restaurants, no interesting job—just heat and dust and hard work.'

It would be hard, Copper thought. There was no doubt about it. And yet Mal's wife would have other things. She would have the creek and the gums and the diamond bright air. She would be able to reach out and touch Mal whenever she wanted. His lean, brown body would be as familiar to her as her own. She'd have long, sweet nights in his arms, and when she went to sleep she would know that he would be there in the morning when she woke. What kind of woman had Lisa been to walk away from all that?

A woman like her? Something cold touched Copper's heart. 'None of that would matter if she loved you,' she said, in a voice that was not quite steady.

'If there's one thing I learnt from my marriage, it's that love isn't enough,' said Mal bleakly. 'Lisa loved me—or she said she did—and look where that got me. And look at you. You love Glyn, but not enough to give up the things that really matter to you. Why should it be any different for the next woman I marry? Always supposing I could find one wandering around the bush! No,' he said, getting to his feet and beginning to untether Megan's pony, 'I'm not getting married again. Megan will be all right if I can find a decent housekeeper. All I can do is keep hoping that one will turn up sooner or later.'

He glanced over his shoulder at his daughter. 'Come on, Megan. We're going home.'

CHAPTER FOUR

'I'M NOT getting married again.' Again and again, over the next few days, Copper found herself brooding over Mal's words, although she could never satisfactorily explain to herself why they grated in her memory so much.

After all, Mal and his daughter weren't her business. It was a shame that his marriage had been such a disaster, of course, but Copper couldn't help resenting the way he had lumped her in the same category as Lisa. *She* hadn't walked out on a marriage, or deprived a father of his child. Glyn was the one who had walked out on her. All she had done was care about the work she did. What was so wrong with that?

At least she understood now the guarded way Mal treated her. He was polite but watchful, and, although he patently found her amusing in an exasperating kind of way, he rarely smiled—and if he did it was as if the smile had been surprised out of him against his will. Sometimes Copper felt his eyes resting on her with an expression that she could never identify, but which made her edgy and nervous, and she wanted to shout at him and tell him that she wasn't like Lisa.

At times, Copper hated Lisa for turning the intriguing man she remembered into this cool, reserved stranger. And at other times, like now, lying awake in the dark, she was disgusted to find herself envying her. Lisa had been beautiful, Mal had said. He must have loved her very much. He had married her and brought her to

Birraminda and done everything he could to make her stay.

Which meant that it hadn't taken long for him to forget *her*. Megan was four and a half now, so he must have married Lisa at least five years ago, six if one took into account the fact that the marriage had gone wrong long before the baby was conceived. And *that* meant that a year after their idyllic encounter on that Mediterranean beach Mal had dismissed her from his mind and married someone else.

Copper turned over irritably. The knowledge that he had so quickly forgotten left her feeling a fool for having remembered him so clearly, even when all hope of ever seeing him again had gone. It was just that the three days they had spent together had felt so utterly right that it was impossible to believe that it hadn't been meant to last for ever. She had used to invent endless excuses as to why Mal had never got in touch with her in London, as he had promised, but never once had she thought that he would simply carry straight on and fall in love with someone else.

Perhaps he had never really been in love with her at all. Perhaps she had just been another girl on another beach. The thought twisted in Copper like a knife.

At least it made it easier for her to pretend that she didn't care about the fact that Mal had obviously dismissed her as an obsessive career woman. Copper told herself that if he wanted to waste his life being suspicious of every woman he met, that was his loss. She just had to persuade him to let Copley Travel use Birraminda as their base and then she would be more than happy to go back to Adelaide and forget him properly this time!

But as the days passed, and a week turned into ten days, Copper began to almost forget why she had come to Birraminda in the first place. She had rung her father to explain that she would be staying on to argue their case properly, but she had stuck to her word and hadn't tried to tackle Mal on the subject.

Most afternoons he took her and Megan for a ride or a drive to more distant parts of the station. For the first few days she rushed around with a clipboard, taking notes and measurements and inspecting the landing strip where Mal kept a small plane, but after a while there seemed to be too much else important to do.

Without daily contact with her office, the business had become increasingly unreal. Real was the dazzling outback light and Megan's face screwed up in concentration. It was the sound of the birds squabbling in the trees and the sway of the saddle and the way Mal creased up his eyes as he scanned the wide, empty horizon.

Copper hated getting up early, and couldn't say that she had learnt to love housework, but she did enjoy being with Megan. She taught her how to write her name and she read her stories and played endless imaginary games, and slowly the little girl began to blossom. It was not all plain sailing, of course. Megan was a bright, funny child, but she had a wilful streak and was prone to tantrums if crossed. She soon discovered, though, that Copper's will was even stronger than her own, and that she could only go so far. Every night Copper would tuck her into bed and kiss her goodnight before Mal came in, and Megan's arms would hug her neck, and that was enough for Copper to feel that the long, exhausting day had been worthwhile.

'Look, Dad, I'm having my hair washed!' Megan stood up in the bath one evening to show off her halo of shampoo and waved her hands excitedly at her father.

Copper had been crouching by the bath, but at that

she jerked round, annoyed to find that after ten days her heart still hadn't learnt not to cartwheel crazily whenever Mal appeared unexpectedly. She had been entertaining Megan by singing with a plastic beaker clamped over her nose, and she was so busy trying to get her breathing under control that she forgot all about it until Mal lifted an enquiring eyebrow. Flushing ridiculously, she snatched the beaker off her face. Why was it that when she tried so hard to be cool and business-like Mal always seemed to find her making a fool of herself?

'You're early,' she said, almost truculently.

'I know,' said Mal with infuriating calmness. 'I thought this might be a good time for you to put your case for a campsite.'

'Oh.' Copper sat back on her heels and pushed her tousled hair behind her ears. Her sleeves were pushed up to her elbows and the beaker had left a faint red mark across the bridge of her nose. 'Now?'

'I'll just have a shower and then I can finish putting Megan to bed while you get your papers together. We could have a talk after that.'

'Fine.' Trust Mal to wait until she had forgotten all her carefully rehearsed arguments and then expect her to convince him with just half an hour's notice!

Well, if he was going to have a shower, she was going to have one too. There was no way Copper was going to face him looking hot and crumpled after a day running round after a four-year-old. This was her big chance and she mustn't blow it.

Copper stood under the streaming water and tried to gear herself back into executive mode. She thought about her father, anxiously awaiting news of Mal's decision, and she thought about Copley Travel's falling bookings. They badly needed a successful new idea to capture people's imagination, and the Birraminda tours could put them back as market leaders in exclusive holidays. There were other properties they could try if Mal refused to be convinced, but her father had his heart set on Birraminda—and anyway, it would take too long to go back to square one at this stage. Mal *had* to say yes!

Copper dressed carefully in a soft cream-coloured outfit made up of a swirling panelled skirt and a neat, cropped top. When she looked at herself in the mirror she thought she looked cool and business-like, more like herself, somehow, but not too smart to alienate Mal before she started. She could hear him putting Megan to bed next door as she left her room with her files under one arm. That meant there would be time for her to go and check the roast.

'You look stunning!' Brett came whistling into the kitchen as she bent down to put the beef back in the oven.

It was impossible not to like Brett. He was selfish and careless and irresponsible, but he flirted outrageously and made Copper laugh even when she most wanted to disapprove. Every time she saw him she was struck by how handsome he was, but his sudden appearance never had the slightest effect on her breathing, and her heart just kept placidly beating—which was strange, considering the ridiculous way it behaved whenever she saw Mal.

Next to Brett, he looked austere and understated, as if deliberately underplaying the warmth and humour that Copper remembered so well from Turkey, and yet there was no doubt who held the authority. Brett might tease his brother, or grumble at his orders, but he never challenged him, and when the men rode out in a group there was something indefinable about Mal that marked him out as leader, although he was never loud or aggressive, nor did he make any effort to draw attention to himself.

Shutting the oven door now, she turned to smile a welcome at Brett, her hands still in the mitts. 'Busy day?'

'Frantic,' said Brett lazily. 'Mal doesn't seem to appreciate that there are only so many hours in one day.' He strolled over to the cooker and lifted the lid of a saucepan to sniff appreciatively. 'Where is the old slave-driver, anyway?'

'He's just putting Megan to bed.'

'Oh, good, so he's out of the way for a bit.' Brett brightened and slid an arm around Copper's waist. 'I never seem to get a chance to talk to you on your own. Mal's always hanging around and watching disapprovingly if I go anywhere near you. Have you noticed?'

Copper had. She noticed everything about Mal. He had made a point of never leaving her alone with Brett, although it must have been obvious that she was in no danger of taking his brother seriously. In another man, his behaviour might have looked like jealousy, but Copper had the nasty feeling that she was the last woman Mal would care about. She was too like Lisa for him to be jealous. He made no effort to charm her, as Brett did, and his eyes when they rested on her held no warmth but only an odd, speculative expression.

'He's got a lot on his mind,' she told Brett, even as she marvelled to find herself defending Mal.

'So have I,' said Brett. 'A pair of gorgeous green eyes that do terrible things to a man's blood pressure.' His hold tightened. 'Has anyone ever told you what an enchanting smile you've got, Copper?'

If Mal had put his arm round her, Copper would have been strumming with nerves, but she didn't even bother to move away from Brett as she laughed up at him. 'Now, why do I get the feeling that you've used that line before?'

Brett grinned. 'I've never meant it before, though! I swear, you're the prettiest girl we've ever had out here and I'm madly in love with you. Why won't you love me back?'

'I've just got no taste,' said Copper, shaking her head in mock sorrow. 'Sad, isn't it?'

'It does seem a waste,' agreed Brett, blue eyes dancing. 'A beautiful girl like you should be in love with someone. You haven't done anything silly like falling in love with Mal, have you? He's a hardened case, and you'd have much more fun with me!'

It was obvious that he was joking, but Copper sprang away from him as if he had jabbed her with a hot poker. 'In love with *Mal*?' she spluttered, with quite unnecessary vehemence. 'What a ridiculous idea! Of course I'm not in love with Mal!'

'Now that we've cleared that up, do you think you could come and say goodnight to Megan?' Mal's cool voice from the doorway made Copper spin round, her cheeks aflame. 'Then, if you're ready, we could have that talk—or are you and Brett busy?'

'No—no, of course not,' stammered Copper, but Brett only grinned.

'Yes, we are,' he said gaily. 'I'm extremely busy trying to persuade Copper to fall in love with me, but so far we've only established that she's not in love with you!'

Mal's expression was unreadable. 'So I heard.'

'I'll—um— I'll just say goodnight to Megan,' said Copper hurriedly. She tried to gather up her files from the kitchen table, but she was so flustered that she managed to drop most of them on the floor, and then had to scrabble around picking them up again.

Mal held the door open for her with ironic courtesy. 'I'll be in my office,' he said.

What did it matter if he had heard her tell Brett that she wasn't in love with him? Copper asked herself as she bent down to kiss Megan. It was perfectly true. OK, there had been Turkey, but that had been youthful infatuation, and anyway, he had been different then. He wasn't in love with her now and she wasn't in love with him.

Absolutely, definitely not.

So why are you lurking in here as if you don't want to face him? an inner voice enquired. Copper drew a deep breath. The whole future of Copley Travel was at stake while she was dithering in here. Stop being pathetic, she told herself. Just go out there and show Mal what you're made of!

'Come in,' said Mal as she knocked at the open door with an assumption of confidence. He came round his desk to shut the door behind her. 'Sit down.'

The formality was a little disconcerting, but Copper took it as encouragement. Mal was just making it clear that this was a business meeting like any other. Trying to ignore the undertow of tension in the room, she opened a file and drew out the plan of the waterhole site that her father had drawn and a sheaf of artists' impressions of what the camp would look like.

She talked for nearly an hour. And all the time she was excruciatingly aware of Mal leaning over the plans, of the taut power of his body close to hers, the brown finger running down a list of figures and the hard, exciting line of his cheek tugging at the edge of her vision.

At length Copper talked herself to a standstill. She

had done the best she could and now all she could do was wait for Mal's decision. 'I'm not sure that there's anything else I can tell you at this stage,' she said carefully as she began to stack the papers back together. 'Obviously there are still a lot of details to be worked out, but at this stage we'd really just like to reach an agreement with you in principle.'

There was no way of telling what he thought of her arguments. His face gave nothing away as he straightened from the desk and walked over to the window. 'This project means a great deal to you, doesn't it?' he said, turning back to face her at last.

'Yes, it does,' she said honestly.

'I'm just wondering how much you're prepared to do to get me to agree to it.'

'Well, the figure I suggested is open to negotiation,' Copper began with caution, but Mal waved that idea aside.

'I'm not talking about money. I'm talking about what you personally are prepared to do.'

'Personally?' What was he driving at? Copper gave a rather uncertain laugh. 'I guess it rather depends on the sort of thing you've got in mind.'

'Let's say marriage, for instance.'

She froze in the middle of shoving papers back into their file, wondering if she had misheard. '*Marriage*? Whose marriage?'

'Yours and mine,' said Mal calmly.

Copper had the oddest feeling that the floor had tipped beneath her feet, and she sat down abruptly on her chair, still clutching the file. 'Is this some kind of joke?' she asked, in a voice that sounded quite unlike her own.

'Believe me, I've never felt less like joking,' said Mal. 'I'm offering you a straight deal. Here it is: you can use the waterhole to do whatever you want with your tourists if you agree to marry me. I'm not talking about a lifetime commitment,' he went on when Copper just gaped at him. 'I'm thinking of an agreed period of three years—but that figure is open to negotiation, as you would say.'

Copper moistened her lips surreptitiously. She couldn't get rid of the feeling that she had blundered into a play to discover that she had no idea of her own lines. 'But—but this is crazy!' she stuttered. 'You don't even want to get married. You said so!'

'I don't *want* to, but I will. I need a wife.' Mal picked up a fax message from a pile on his desk. 'I got this from the agency today. They've found a girl who's prepared to come out on a short-term contract, but I can see already what's going to happen. She'll be keen for a week or so and then she'll get bored, and Brett will think it's his duty to entertain her, and before we know where we are she'll be in tears and booking herself on the first bus back to Brisbane. Meanwhile Megan is left, abandoned by yet another stranger just when she's got used to her.'

He dropped the fax wearily back onto the desk. 'I've been thinking about what you said at the waterhole that day, and I've decided that you're right.'

'Something *I* said?' echoed Copper, surprise helping her to find her voice. 'What did I say?'

'You said that marriage didn't have to be the way it was with Lisa, and the more I think about it, the more I think you're right. A business arrangement where both sides know quite clearly what's involved would be a different sort of marriage altogether.'

'That wasn't exactly the different kind of marriage I had in mind,' she said with a tiny sigh, but Mal wasn't listening.

'It makes sense,' he said, getting up to prowl around the room as he ticked the advantages off on his fingers. 'Even Brett would draw the line at seducing his brother's wife, so I get a permanent housekeeper and Megan gets a mother figure. Three years isn't ideal, but it's more security than she gets at the moment, and—who knows?—the marriage might be a success and we could renegotiate terms for a longer period.'

'I don't believe this!' said Copper incredulously. 'You're not seriously asking me to marry you just to solve your housekeeping problems?'

'Why not? You're perfect.' Mal stopped striding and came to prop himself against the desk beside her so that he could study her dispassionately. 'The first and most important thing is that you're good with Megan and she likes you.'

'I'm not being asked to marry Megan, though, am I?'

'Second,' he said, ignoring her sarcastic interruption, 'you don't seem to take Brett too seriously. And third, as you were so busy telling Brett, you're not in love with me.'

Copper looked down at the file in her lap. She was very aware of the soft material of her skirt hanging against her bare legs and there was a cold knot gathering deep inside her. 'Most husbands would think of that as a disadvantage,' she said, amazed that she could sound so composed when her blood was still booming at the shock of his proposal.

'It's not as far as I'm concerned,' said Mal. 'I've had one wife who said she loved me, and I don't want another. No, you've told me that you're not romantic, and that suits me fine. I want someone who'll treat the marriage like a business deal, with no messy emotions or false expectations of what it'll be like.'

'And what do I get out of this *deal*?'

He looked at her in surprise. 'I would have thought that was obvious. You get the chance to run your business at Birraminda. You can say what you like about group leaders and logistical operations, but when it comes down to it, a project that size is going to have to have someone permanently on the spot. Just organising supplies is going to be a full-time job, and who's going to deal with your people when they turn up at Birraminda wanting gas or a telephone or someone to mend a tyre? You can't do any of that from Adelaide, so you might as well be up here yourself, keeping an eye on everything.'

'It's a big step from administrator to wife,' Copper pointed out, still hardly able to credit that they were actually *talking* about the crazy idea.

'You can look on it as doing two jobs at the same time,' said Mal. 'It's not even as if I'm asking you to choose between your husband and your business, am I?' He folded his arms across his chest, about at Copper's eye level, and she found herself staring at the dark hairs on his forearms where his blue checked shirt was rolled up from his wrists.

'Look,' he went on, as if talking about the most reasonable thing in the world, 'I wouldn't have thought of suggesting it if you hadn't told me how things were in Adelaide. As it is, you're alone, your boyfriend's gone off with someone else and your friends are feeling uncomfortable. Marrying me would be the perfect excuse to move away for a while.'

'You don't think marriage is rather an extreme solution to a bit of awkwardness?' Copper asked, her tone edged with irony. 'I could get a job in another state if I was that desperate to get away.'

'I'm offering you that job,' he said. 'You don't have to be madly in love to work successfully with someone.'

'No, but it helps when you're married to them!'

'Not in my experience.' The corners of Mal's mouth turned down. 'You've said that all you're really interested in is your business. Well, that's fine by me—I'm offering you the chance to prove it. You can stay here as my wife and make sure that your project is a success or you can find some other station owner willing to put up with all the hassle. Either way, I'd bet that you're going to spend most of your time sorting out problems on site, so you might as well be here at Birraminda where you'd have a lot more influence.'

Copper sat bolt upright. 'Can we get this quite clear?' she said coldly. 'You'll let Copley Travel use Birraminda if I agree to marry you, but if not, the whole project's off?'

'That's it,' he agreed, as if pleased with her quick comprehension.

'But that's blackmail!'

Mal shrugged. 'I prefer to look on it as a question of priorities. I've already decided mine—Megan. All you have to do is decide what yours is.'

It was a challenge. Angry green eyes stared into impassive brown in an almost audible clash of wills, while the air between them jangled with tension. Copper didn't know whether she wanted to laugh or cry or simply haul off and hit him for standing there so coolly while she felt as if the whole world was reeling. All she knew was that if her father's dreams weren't to fall apart there and then, she couldn't throw Mal's offer back in his face with the contempt it deserved and stalk out of the room.

Her gaze dropped and she lurched to her feet. 'I—I'll

have to think about it,' she said, gathering the rest of her files from the desk with fumbling fingers.

'All right.' Mal levered himself upright as well and walked over to open the door for her. 'Let me know when you've made a decision,' he said, and shut the door behind her.

That was it? Copper stared incredulously at the closed door, her files clutched in her arms. No word of encouragement, no suggestion of reassurance, no attempt at persuasion. Would it have killed him to show a little more interest in her? Mal was obviously never going to declare undying love after his first marriage, but he could have said that he found her attractive or that he liked her, or even just that he felt they would get on together. That would have been better than nothing. At least it wouldn't have left her feeling as if her most important attributes in his eyes were availability and a susceptibility to blackmail!

Anyway, the whole idea was ridiculous. She would say no, of course. Of course she would.

Copper was distracted through dinner, oblivious to Brett's teasing comments about what she and Mal had been up to in the office for so long, and aware only of Mal sitting at the head of the table. If he was worried about her decision, he gave absolutely no sign of it. He must have known that she would still be reeling after his extraordinary proposal, but did he make the slightest effort to make her feel as if he cared one way or the other? A smile, a reassuring look, even an effort to include her in the conversation was all it would take, but no! He just sat there and talked about *cows*. She wasn't even going to *think* about marrying him!

The trouble was that she *was* thinking about it, Copper realised as she tossed and turned in futile search of sleep that night. On her way to bed, she had checked automatically on Megan. A restless sleeper, she always ended up sprawled half-in and half-out of bed. Copper straightened her and tucked the bedclothes around her, stroking the soft curls away from the child's face. Megan mumbled in her sleep and sighed and Copper felt her heart contract. Maybe there were worse ways to spend three years than in making sure that a child was loved and secure.

She had thought, too, about going back to England to work for a couple of years once the Birraminda project was up and running. They had recently recruited a promising new member of staff to run the agency office, so she would hardly be abandoning her father. It would give her a break from Adelaide and the humiliating sympathy of friends. Why shouldn't she spend those years at Birraminda instead? What difference would it make?

Mal would make the difference. The very thought of marrying him clutched at the base of Copper's spine. You couldn't live with someone for three years and not become part of their life. 'A business arrangement', Mal had said, but just how business-like did he intend their marriage to be? Would they calmly go off to their separate rooms at night, as they did now, or would they share a room? Would he expect her to go to sleep lying next to him every night, to wake up next to him every morning? That was what a real wife would do—but then, Mal didn't want a real wife, Copper remembered bleakly.

Or did he? Housekeeper or wife—which did he really want? And which could she bear to be?

Copper fell into an exhausted sleep at last, surprised to find when she woke that she felt much calmer. She was even able to have a cool discussion with Mal about what time they would be back from the muster that eve-

ning and whether or not Naomi would provide sandwiches for their lunch. The really important issue, she
had woken up realising, was not whether Mal would
sleep with her or not, but the effect on her father if she
refused to marry him and he carried out his threat to
deny them access to Birraminda.

Dan would be bitterly disappointed at losing what he
considered the perfect site. He would be frustrated at the
delay in getting the project off the ground, and depressed
at the thought of starting again and finding somewhere
else. Already desperately worried about the future of
Copley Travel if they couldn't break into a new market,
the last thing her father needed at the moment was the
additional stress of seeing his beloved project crumbling
before his eyes. If she went home without Mal's agreement, Copper would feel that she had failed him miserably, and she already knew what that felt like.

Once before, fresh out of college, she had had a choice
between spending two years working and travelling in
Europe, or helping her father out at the agency during a
particularly difficult period. Dan had urged Copper to go
while she had the chance, and it had been the best time
of her life, but her father had soldiered on alone and
when he had had his first heart attack everyone had been
surprised that it hadn't happened sooner. Copper,
though, just back from England, had never forgiven herself. It wouldn't have killed her to have put off her trip
for a few months, but it had nearly killed her father, who
had loved her and protected her and cared for her, just
as Mal did his own daughter.

No, she had failed her father once, but she wouldn't
do it again.

Megan was ensconced at the kitchen table, breathing
heavily over a work of art provisionally entitled 'Two

Horses in a Paddock'. An identical scribble, which Copper had assumed was a third horse, was scornfully described by the artist as 'a house—no, a crocodile—no, it's Dad', which just went to show how much Copper knew.

Copper couldn't help thinking that a house or even a crocodile would be a lot easier to deal with than the particular dad in question as she dialled her parents' number on her mobile phone. She wasn't going to ask their advice—they would be appalled if they knew what she was considering—but she needed to talk to them before she made up her mind one way or the other.

'Dad's *much* better,' said Jill Copley in answer to Copper's determinedly casual enquiry. She lowered her voice so that Dan couldn't hear from the bedroom, where he was resting. 'You know what a worrier he is, and he'd been fretting about what would happen if you didn't manage to set up this deal with Matthew Standish, but ever since you rang and told us you were staying on up there for a while he's been so much more relaxed. He seemed to think that it was a good sign and he's been driving me mad with plans for once the site's agreed. I haven't seen him this positive for a long time,' she confided. 'It's done him so much good and we're both so grateful to you, dear.'

'Mal—Mr Standish—hasn't committed himself to any definite agreement yet,' Copper said. She felt she had to warn her, but her mother was apparently in as confident a mood as her father.

'He'd hardly say no when you've been up there nearly two weeks, would he? What's he like, anyway?' she went on, before Copper could answer. 'Your father's not much help. He just says he's no fool. Is he nice?'

An image of Mal burned behind Copper's eyelids: the

stern angles of his face, the impenetrable brown eyes, the corners of his mouth that dented into something that was almost but not quite a smile, the way he picked up his daughter, the way he rode his horse, the way he settled his hat on his head. 'He can be.'

'Is he married?'

Copper hesitated. 'No.'

'Ah.' Her mother managed to invest it with at least six syllables, not to mention a question mark and an exclamation mark.

'Don't be silly, Mum,' said Copper, a little too sharply. 'Is Dad there?'

Dan was delighted to hear from her, and was bubbling over with so many plans that Copper had a hard time getting a word in edgeways. 'Now, how are you getting on with Matthew Standish?' he asked buoyantly at last. 'Have we got to the stage where we can start drawing up a contract yet?'

Copper looked at Megan's dark head bent over her picture, and then at the phone in her hand. 'Just one or two details to sort out, Dad,' she said slowly, 'and then we'll be ready to sign.'

'Good girl!' Dan was bursting with pride and excitement. 'I knew you wouldn't let me down.'

'No,' said Copper almost to herself as she pressed the button to cut the connection. 'I won't let you down, Dad.' Very carefully, she pushed the antenna back into place and laid the phone on the table.

It looked as if her decision was made.

CHAPTER FIVE

COPPER edged warily around the holding yards, eyeing the milling cattle with distinct nervousness. She had watched, awed, from the verandah as they had come pounding in a cloud of snorting, stamping red dust. It was hard to believe that so many animals could be controlled by a mere six men on horses, but now, a couple of hours later, they were all firmly corralled and the noise and confusion had slowly subsided to an occasional aggrieved bellow.

Two of the jackaroos were perched laconically on a fence, enjoying a smoke with the satisfaction of a job well done. 'Have you seen Mal?' she asked.

'Last time I saw him, he was heading towards the paddock,' said one out of the corner of his mouth.

So he *was* back. Copper's mouth tightened. It was two days since Mal's proposal—or rather, his ultimatum—and since then he had made no effort to get her on her own. Copper had been gripped by a kind of nervous energy after making her decision, and all she'd wanted was to tell Mal so that she could stop thinking about whether it was the right one or not. But they had been out mustering in the far paddocks yesterday and had slept in their swags under the stars. This was her first chance to talk to him.

Copper had been tense all day, waiting for him to come home, and since she had heard them come in her nerves had reached snapping point. But Mal, it seemed, was in no hurry to find out what she had decided, and

in the end she had come in search of him herself, unable
to bear the waiting any longer.

The paddock where the horses were kept was irrigated, and in the late afternoon light, it looked peaceful
and still and very green in contrast to the red dust around
it. Copper could see Duke grazing in the shade, flicking
his tail against the inevitable flies, and she called his
name, absurdly gratified to see his head come up. He
gazed at her for a moment with liquid brown eyes and
then calmly resumed his placid chewing, having obviously decided that it wasn't worth the bother of coming
over to say hello.

He and Mal had a lot in common, thought Copper
with an inward sigh, and turned away from the fence
only to see Mal himself coming round the corner of the
paddock on his great chestnut, Red.

The paddock, the yards, the dusty track beneath her
feet all dropped abruptly into nothingness, and there was
only Mal, very distinct against the blue outback sky.
Copper felt oddly weightless, suspended in thin air, and
something clutched at her heart as the nerves that had
buoyed her up all day collapsed into sudden shyness.
Two whole days she had been waiting to talk to him,
and now that he was here, she couldn't think of anything
to say.

'Hello,' was all she managed, shading her eyes against
the glare with one hand as he brought Red to a halt in
front of her.

High up on the horse, Mal seemed impossibly remote
and unapproachable as he looked down at Copper, standing slender in jeans and a pale, long-sleeved T-shirt. The
sunlight glanced off her thick brown hair, turning it to
bronze, and tipped her lashes with gold. Very conscious
of his scrutiny, Copper found that she couldn't look back

at him. Instead she stroked Red's nose and fiddled with his bridle.

'Where's Megan?' asked Mal after a moment.

'I left her with Naomi.' Bill, the "married man", and his wife had two toddlers and another baby on the way, and when Copper had seen how tired Naomi looked she had felt rather guilty about asking her if she could keep an eye on Megan for a few minutes. 'I...I wanted to talk to you on our own.'

'About our marriage?'

'Yes.'

Without a word, Mal swung easily off the horse and led it into the paddock. Copper had to wait and watch as he took off the bridle and hung the saddle over the fence. The men were notoriously unsentimental about the animals they worked with, but she was oddly touched to see that Mal fed Red something from his shirt pocket and let the big horse nuzzle his arm before he gave it a final pat and a slap on the rump to send it cantering off into the field.

Only then did he close the gate behind him and join Copper where she stood watching the way Red kicked up his heels and revelled in his freedom. He leant his arms on the fence and glanced at her from under his dusty hat.

'Well?' he said.

'There's no need to sound so anxious to find out what I've decided,' snapped Copper, whose nerves had snarled up again as soon as Mal came near her.

Mal sighed. 'What would be the point of me getting in a state about it?' he asked. 'Nothing I can do is going to change your mind, whatever you've decided.'

'That's good coming from a man who wrapped up a proposal of marriage in a neat bit of blackmail!'

'It wasn't blackmail,' said Mal evenly. 'It's your choice whether you marry me or not.'

'Some choice!' muttered Copper.

His eyes rested on the grazing horses beneath the trees. 'Are you trying to tell me that your answer's no?'

'Are you sure you can be bothered to hear the answer?' she retorted, and he frowned.

'What do you mean by that?'

'You make me a bizarre offer of marriage and then ignore me for the next two days,' she accused him. 'Hardly the action of a man who's particularly interested one way or another!'

Mal's jaw tightened ominously. 'I've been mustering for the last two days,' he pointed out. 'How could I ignore you when I wasn't even here?'

'You ignored me all evening before you left,' Copper countered sullenly. '*And* this afternoon! You've been back for hours but you never even tried to find me!'

'I've been back just over half an hour,' said Mal, tight-lipped. 'I brought in the stragglers at the rear, so I've only just got them in and finished checking the others. That hasn't left me much time to ignore you, but, since you ask, even if I'd got back with the others I wouldn't have rushed straight up to the homestead to demand an answer only to be accused of pressurising you! I reckoned you needed time to think things through and I was prepared to wait until you were ready to tell me what you'd decided.' His voice acquired a certain steel. 'Now that you *are* ready—presumably—perhaps you could tell me what you've decided. Or am I expected to guess?'

'Under the circumstances, that shouldn't be too hard,' she snapped back without thinking.

At least she had the satisfaction of provoking Mal to

exasperation. 'Look, Copper, why don't you just give me your answer?' He sighed. 'Are you going to marry me or not? Yes or no?'

There was a pause. This wasn't how the conversation had been meant to go, Copper thought desperately. She had intended to be cool and crisply business-like and look what had happened! She had ended up sounding like a petulant child instead.

She scuffed one foot against the bottom rail of the fence. 'Yes,' she muttered. Oh, God, she still sounded like Megan after a tantrum. She cleared her throat. 'Yes, I will marry you,' she said more clearly. 'But only if you sign a formal agreement allowing Copley Travel access and control over the site.'

'Fine,' said Mal.

Copper waited for more, but apparently that was it. 'Fine?' she repeated, her voice rising in outrage. '*Fine*? Is that all you can say?'

'What else do you want me to say? I've got no objection to a formal agreement—quite the opposite. I suggest that before we get married we get a legal contract drawn up that specifies the conditions that we've both agreed to in advance. I'm not risking another divorce settlement like last time, so when we agree a date to end the marriage, we can agree the financial implications as well.'

'I don't want your money,' said Copper with distaste. 'All I'll want is assurance that Copley Travel can continue to use Birraminda after the marriage is over.'

'That's something that can be discussed when we draw up the contract,' said Mal indifferently. 'All I'm saying is that we should know exactly where we stand before we get married. I'm sure a woman of your business acumen will see the sense in a legal contract.'

The prospect of reducing a marriage to a number of clauses in a contract chilled Copper to the bone, but, having brought up the idea of a written agreement, she was hardly in a position to object. 'Right now I think we've got more important things to discuss than a prenuptial contract,' she said.

'Like what?'

'Like...well, like *everything*!' said Copper in frustration. She lifted her arms and then let them drop helplessly to her sides. 'For a start, what are we going to tell everybody?'

Mal turned so that he was leaning back against the fence and considered her. 'We just tell them we're getting married,' he said, and Copper hugged her arms together edgily.

'We'll need to do more than that to convince my parents that I'm serious about going to live with a perfect stranger! They'd be horrified if they knew why we're getting married,' she pointed out. 'I'll only marry you on the condition that they never, ever guess what I'm doing—and that means convincing them that we're a genuine couple.'

'What's a *genuine* couple?' asked Mal with a sardonic look. 'Every marriage is different, so why should we be any less genuine than the others?'

'You know what I mean!' said Copper crossly. 'My parents need to believe that we're getting married because we're madly in love, not because we've agreed some cold-blooded business deal.'

Mal hooked his thumbs into the pockets of his dust-encrusted jeans. 'That's not a problem, is it?'

How could he sound so casual about it? Copper eyed him resentfully. 'No, but I'm wondering how good your acting is!'

'We're both going to have to get used to acting,' said Mal, unperturbed. 'There's no point to the whole exercise unless everyone believes that you're a suitably loving wife—particularly Brett. Do you think you'll be able to convince him that you're more interested in me than you are in your business?'

'That depends on whether you'll be able to convince him that *you're* a suitably loving husband,' she said tartly.

'I expect I can manage that.'

Copper was stung by his laconic attitude. They might have been discussing the chances of rain—although, come to think of it, Mal would probably get a lot more excited about *that*! 'There's a bit more to marriage than just behaving affectionately in front of other people, you know! I think we should establish now just how "married" we're going to be. Real wives aren't just housekeepers with rings on their fingers,' she went on with some difficulty. 'They share things with their husbands in private as well as in public…like bedrooms, for instance.'

'We're not likely to persuade Brett that you belong with me unless we share a bedroom,' Mal agreed dryly. 'And a bed.' He glanced at Copper, who was picking a splinter of wood out of the fence post, her face averted. 'Or is that the problem?'

'It's not a *problem*,' Copper said, flustered now that she had finally come to the point. She pushed her hair awkwardly behind her ears. 'It's just…well, yes, I think we should decide now whether…you know, whether you…whether *we*…'

She could hear herself floundering and risked a peep at Mal. There was the faintest suggestion of a smile bracketing his mouth. That meant he knew exactly what she was trying to say but wasn't going to make it any easier for her. He was just leaning back against the rail, looking cool and calm and completely relaxed and watching her with those infuriatingly unreadable brown eyes. A spurt of real anger helped Copper pull herself together and she turned to face him directly.

'What I'm trying to ask,' she said icily, 'is whether you're expecting us to sleep together?'

'Why not?' said Mal with the same aggravating calmness.

'Well, we…we hardly know each other.'

'That didn't stop us before, did it?'

There was a long, long silence. Copper froze and then, very slowly, she turned her head to look at him. 'So you do remember!'

'Did you think I'd forgotten?' There was an enigmatic look in Mal's brown eyes, and a faint smile touched his mouth.

'Why didn't you say anything before?' she asked huskily. She felt very peculiar, as if the past and the present had suddenly collapsed together into a jumble of conflicting emotions where nothing was certain any more.

'You didn't.' With a shrug Mal turned back to watch the horses. 'I wasn't sure at first. I recognised your name as soon as Megan told me, but you looked so different,' he said slowly, as if visualising the Copper who had stood clutching the verandah post and comparing her with the girl who had walked out of the crowd towards him across the sand.

Her hair had been longer then, dishevelled from the sea and streaked with sunshine, and like almost everyone else on her tour she had worn shorts and a faded sleeveless top. Only her smile had marked her out from the ordinary—her smile and the clear green eyes that had looked so directly into his.

'Your hair's shorter now—smarter, I suppose,' he went on after a moment. 'You had sunglasses on, you were wearing a suit, for God's sake, and I simply wasn't expecting you. It hardly seemed possible that you could be the same girl. And then you took off your sunglasses and I saw your eyes and I realised that it really was you. By then...'

Mal paused, lifting his shoulders as if searching for the best way to explain. 'Well, by then it was clear that even if you had recognised me, you weren't going to acknowledge it. I don't know—I thought you might feel awkward, even embarrassed about working for me if I raised the subject, and since I was assuming that you'd come as a new housekeeper it just seemed easier to follow your lead and pretend that you were a stranger.' He glanced sideways at Copper. 'It's been seven years, after all,' he added. 'There was no reason why you should have remembered me.'

No reason? Copper thought about his lips against her skin, about the mastery of his hands and the sleek, supple strength of his body. She thought about the way he had made her senses sing and the breathtaking passion they had shared.

She wanted to look at the horses, at the fence, at her hands, at anything other than Mal, but an irresistible force was dragging her gaze round and against her will she found herself looking into his eyes, drowning in the brown depths that sucked her into the past, sending her spinning back seven years to the moment when she had looked up, laughing, from the crowd and seen him watching her.

Mal had been travelling on his own, Copper with a

group due to move on in three days, but none of that had mattered at the time. They had been more than just fellow Australians far from home; they had been two halves of a whole, clicking naturally into place. Being together had seemed utterly right, as if it had been somehow inevitable that they should meet that way. It was like a compass swinging to north, like an arrow heading straight for its target, like walking through a door and knowing that you had come home without even realising that you had been away.

It had been time out of time. For three days they had talked and laughed. They had swum in the turquoise sea. Droplets of water had glistened on Mal's shoulders as he surfaced and he had smiled as he shook the wet hair out of his eyes and reached for her. They had climbed the hill to the ruined fort overlooking the beach and watched the sunset, and when the soft night had closed around them making love had been the most natural thing in the world. Afterwards they had walked down to the sea again, to sink into the cool, dark water, and the phosphorescence had glimmered around their entwined bodies.

'Stay,' Mal had said on the last night, but Copper had been part of an overland tour making its way back to London, where friends were expecting her. It hadn't seemed so bad saying goodbye when he had her contact address there and promised to ring her as soon as he got there himself. She had been so sure that they had been meant for each other. How was she to have known that it would be seven years before she saw him again?

No reason to remember him? With an effort, Copper wrenched her eyes from Mal and back to the present. The beach snapped into a dirt track, the warm Mediterranean night into the fierce glare of an outback

afternoon, and she was left feeling jarred and disorientated by the abrupt transition. 'Of course I remembered,'
she said in a low voice.

'Why didn't *you* say anything?'

'The same sort of reasons, I suppose,' she said
weakly. 'I didn't think you remembered *me*. All I knew
was that you'd been married and that your wife had died,
so it didn't seem very appropriate to remind you that
we'd met before. And there didn't seem much point. It
was just a holiday romance,' she added, trying to convince herself.

'Was it?' said Mal, without looking at her.

'You never got in touch,' Copper reminded him. She
wanted to sound casual, as if she hadn't really cared one
way or the other, but her voice came out flat, accusing.

'I rang you,' he said.

Surprise made her swing round. 'No, you didn't!'

'I did,' he insisted. Linking his hands loosely together,
he leant on the top rail once more. Copper could see the
dust on his skin, the pulse beating below his ear. 'I'd
spent that year working as an agricultural consultant in
East Africa. I'd waited until Brett had finished school
and could help Dad while I was away and knew I would
never have a better chance to travel than when my contract was finished. I was making the most of that chance
in Turkey because I knew that once I got back there
wouldn't be many opportunities like it, but it meant that
I was out of contact for a couple of months.'

Mal's voice lost all expression. 'When I got to London
there was a message saying that my father had died suddenly over a month before. Brett was too young to manage on his own so I had to get the first plane home.' He
hesitated. 'I rang you from the airport. One of your

friends answered the phone. She said you were at a party but that she'd give you the message. Didn't you get it?'

'No,' said Copper slowly, thinking how differently she might have felt if she had known that Mal had tried to contact her. 'No, I never got a message.'

'I even tried to ring you from here when I got back,' Mal went on after a moment. 'But you were out again and…oh, I don't know.' He stopped, narrowing his eyes at the distant horizon. 'I suppose there didn't seem much point, just like you said. You were on the other side of the world and obviously having a good time. I remembered what you'd said about your life in Adelaide, about the parties and the clubs and the sailing weekends, and I couldn't see you giving all that up for the kind of life I could offer you out here. I had other things on my mind as well, trying to get Birraminda back together after my father's death.'

He paused again and brought his eyes back to Copper's face. 'You'd seemed like the kind of girl who would enjoy herself whatever she was doing, so I didn't think you would waste much time wondering what had happened to me.'

Only seven years. 'No,' said Copper.

'Anyway,' Mal finished, 'it doesn't matter now. It's all in the past.'

'Yes,' said Copper.

There was an uncomfortable silence. At least *she* found it uncomfortable. Mal didn't look as if it bothered him in the least. It ought to be so easy now that each knew that the other remembered. It ought to be easy to relax, to laugh, to say 'Do you remember?' or 'We had a good time, didn't we?' But somehow it wasn't easy at all. Memories shimmered in the air between them, so close that Copper felt as if she could reach out and push them apart with her hands.

'It's...er...quite a coincidence, isn't it?' she managed at last, moving a few surreptitious inches away from Mal. 'Ending up together again after all this time, I mean.'

'Does it make any difference?' he asked coolly, and she knew that he wasn't thinking of the past but of the present, of Megan and his determination to provide her with stability for as long as he could.

'No,' said Copper awkwardly. She ought to be thinking of the present too, of the future and what this marriage would gain for Copley Travel. 'No, of course not.'

Mal's eyes rested on her standing rigidly away from him, her arms hugged together in an unconsciously defensive posture. 'As far as I'm concerned, as long as you behave like a wife in public after we're married, how you behave in private is your decision. My feeling is that we're both adults, and we've found each other attractive in the past, so we might as well make the most of the time we're going to spend together in bed as well as out of it. We did before.'

'It was different then,' she said with a touch of desperation. '*We're* different. You hadn't been married then; I hadn't met Glyn. It can't ever be the same as it was then.'

Mal's eyes flickered at the mention of Glyn. 'I'm not saying it would be the same,' he said a little impatiently. 'I'm just suggesting that since we're going to be sharing a bed for three years we should enjoy a physical as well as a business relationship, but it's entirely up to you. I won't lay a finger on you in private unless invited. All you have to do is ask...nicely, of course!'

Copper tensed at the undercurrent of mockery in his

voice. 'Will I have to put in a formal request?' she snapped, wishing she had never raised the subject in the first place.

'I'm sure you'll know just what to say if the occasion arises,' said Mal, but when she only scowled at the horses standing companionably nose to tail in the shade, he sighed. 'Look, I can see you don't like the idea. Fine. I respect that. We can even put it in the contract, if that makes you feel any better. As far as I'm concerned, the matter's closed, but if you change your mind, you only have to say so. Until you do, there's no need for you to feel nervous about climbing into bed beside me. Is that clear enough for you?'

'Yes,' said Copper stiltedly. 'Thank you.' Mal's assurance that he wouldn't touch her unless she asked should have been reassuring, but somehow it only made her feel worse. She could hardly object to his willingness to make the choice hers, but he hadn't sounded as if he cared much one way or the other. Did he really expect her to coolly ask him to make love to her?

Copper tried to imagine herself putting in a casual request. Oh, by the way, Mal, I want you to make love to me tonight. Or maybe he had an unspoken invitation in mind? Perhaps he expected her to roll over to his side of the bed and trail her fingers suggestively over his body?

And what would Mal do then? He hadn't exactly fallen over himself to persuade her that they would be as good together as they had been before. He might sigh and shake her off, or—worse—turn over with a martyred air and apply himself to the tedious business of satisfying her. Copper burned with humiliation at the thought. She would never be able to do it! But how could she spend three years sleeping beside him and never touch-

ing him while their memories made a taunting third in
the bed?

'So,' said Mal, settling his hat on his head as he
straightened. 'Do we have a deal?'

Three years keeping house or driving home to tell her
father that she had failed him again? Three years with
Mal or the rest of her life without him? 'Yes,' she said
after a tiny pause. 'We have a deal.'

Mal hadn't missed that moment of hesitation. 'Your
business must mean a lot to you,' he commented with a
sardonic look, and she knew that he was thinking of
Lisa, who had also put business first.

Well, what did it matter if he thought she was just
like his wife? Wasn't that better than letting him know
that she was afraid of the treacherous clamour of her
own body more than anything he might do? 'It does,'
she said, gathering the vestiges of her pride around her
and with only a trace of huskiness in her voice. 'I would
hardly have agreed to marry you if it didn't, would I?'

'No,' he said. 'I suppose you wouldn't.'

Another painful pause. Couldn't he see how desperate
she was for reassurance? Why couldn't he put his arms
around her and tell her that everything would work out
all right? How could he just stand there and *look* like
that when all she wanted was to take two steps and burrow into his hard strength?

'Come on,' said Mal, suddenly brusque. He took off
his hat, ran his fingers through his hair and then put it
back on. 'There's no point in standing here all evening.'

They turned and began walking along the track in the
direction of the homestead, keeping a careful distance
between them. Mal walked with a kind of loose-jointed
ease, so tall and strong that the impulse to scuttle over
and clamp herself to his side like iron to a magnet was

almost irresistible. Copper felt as if she was having to lean away from him in order to walk upright at all.

'When shall we get married?' she asked with a brittle smile, as much to distract herself as anything else.

'The sooner the better, as far as I'm concerned,' said Mal. 'You don't want to make a fuss about the wedding, do you?'

'I wouldn't if it was up to me, but I'm going to have to convince my parents that we're marrying for love, and I think a proper wedding would help. We can keep it small, of course, but they would think it looked suspicious if I didn't get married from home.'

'I suppose it would be more convincing,' he admitted without enthusiasm. 'You're not thinking of long white dresses and veils or anything like that, are you?'

'Of course not.' Copper gritted her teeth at his lack of interest. 'I'm sure I'll be able to find something appropriate to wear. Megan might like to be a bridesmaid, too. I'm just talking about going through the motions, that's all.'

'Well, I'll leave that side of it up to you,' said Mal casually. 'Just tell me when and where I have to turn up.'

'It's nice to know that our wedding is going to mean so much to you,' she said with heavy sarcasm. 'Nobody's going to think that our marriage is genuine if that's going to be your attitude!'

'Oh, don't worry, I'll be suitably loving when required,' he promised.

Copper glanced at him and then away. The sky was flushed with an unearthly pink light as the sun dropped behind the ghost gums lining the creek. 'Do you think anyone will believe that we're really getting married?'

she asked abruptly, as if the words had been forced out of her.

'Why shouldn't they?'

'Well...I've only been up here two weeks. It might all seem a bit sudden.'

'We'll just have to persuade them that we fell in love at first sight, then, won't we?'

We did before. Mal didn't actually say it, but the words hung unspoken in the air between them. They seemed to whisper down Copper's spine and echo in her brain, and in spite of herself a slow, hot flush seeped upwards from her toes.

'Brett's not going to believe that,' she said, keeping her eyes fixed firmly on the sunset. 'He's been with us all the time and he must know quite well that we *haven't* fallen in love. I even told him so the other night.'

'I remember,' said Mal in a dry voice. 'But he didn't believe you. He told me that you were protesting too much.'

Copper stopped dead in the middle of the track. 'Oh, did he?' she said wrathfully.

'Judging by the remarks he was dropping after we'd spent so long in the office that evening, I'd say that he's almost expecting it,' Mal went on calmly. 'All you need to do is go in now looking as if you've just been thoroughly kissed.'

'And how am I supposed to do that?' demanded Copper, distinctly ruffled. 'It's not that easy!'

'Oh, I don't know.' Mal's eyes lit with a sudden speculative gleam and he reached out with one hand, letting his fingers drift tantalisingly down her cheek to curve below her jaw and slide beneath her soft hair. 'I don't think it should be that difficult.'

Copper's heart stilled and she forgot to breathe. She

had emptied of awkwardness, of anger, of any feeling at all except the deep, low thrill that went through her in response to his touch, so that instead of stepping back, or pushing his hand away, she could only stand, her eyes wide and unfocused with a terrible longing. And when Mal put out his other hand to draw her slowly towards him, she went, unresisting.

'In my experience, the simplest solution is usually the best,' he murmured. 'And the simplest way to look kissed is to be kissed,' he added very softly, and then, bending his head, he kissed her at last.

At the first touch of his mouth, a tiny sigh of release escaped Copper, and her lips parted as past and present arrowed into a piercing recognition that this was what she had thought about ever since Mal had walked around the woolshed and back into her life. It was like coming home. His tongue was so enticing, his lips as warm and persuasive as she remembered, but this time the unbearable sweetness that had lingered in her memory for seven long years was swamped almost at once by a great, rolling wave of explosive excitement that caught her unprepared and swept her up into a turbulent tide of desire.

Helpless against it, almost panic-stricken by the sheer force of her response, Copper clutched at Mal's shirt as if trying to anchor herself to the solid security of his body. The dust and the light, the very earth beneath her feet had vanished, leaving her weightless, adrift in a world where nothing existed but Mal—the taste of his mouth, the touch of his hands and the searing intensity of his kiss.

Her body was pounding, her head whirling, and when Mal let go of her face to gather her more closely into his arms she didn't even think to protest. Instead her fingers released their frantic grip on his shirt and crept around his waist, spreading over his back as if impelled by a force of their own.

Their kisses were deep, breathless, almost desperate as the doubts and confusion of the last two weeks swirled away, and all that mattered was the feel of Mal's hands, hard and possessive against her, and his taut male strength, gloriously *real* again after so many years of mere memories. Copper was lost, but she didn't care. She cared only that his arms were around her and that he was kissing her and that she never wanted him to let her go.

CHAPTER SIX

'MAL? Are you—?' Brett's voice broke through the dizzying pleasure that had them in its thrall. It stopped abruptly as he took in the scene. 'Uh-oh!' he said, and, even lost in a different world as she was, Copper could hear him grinning.

Mal didn't even tense. Without haste, he lifted his head and looked at his brother. 'What is it?' he asked, with not so much as a tremor in his voice.

Copper, dazed and shaken, almost fell as he made to release her, and if he hadn't tightened one arm around her once more she was sure that she would simply have collapsed in a heap on the track. Her legs were trembling uncontrollably and her cheeks burned. She couldn't have spoken if she had tried.

'I was coming to see if you were ready for a beer,' said Brett, still grinning broadly. 'But I can see that you're busy!'

'We were until you interrupted us,' said Mal. How could he sound so normal? Copper's heart was pounding, her head spinning, her body aroused and gasping for air, and he wasn't even out of breath!

Brett refused to take the hint. 'I thought it was my job to kiss the housekeepers,' he said, pretending to sound aggrieved.

'Not this housekeeper.' Mal glanced down at Copper, who was still struggling to adjust to the abrupt return to reality. 'This one's mine.'

He looked back at his brother and his voice held a

94

distinct note of warning. 'Copper's going to marry me, so you'll just have to count her as the one that got away.'

'I knew it!' Brett gave a shout of laughter and bounded forward to slap his brother on the shoulder and sweep Copper into an exuberant hug. 'I knew it! Mal thinks I can't read that poker face of his, but I could tell how he felt about you right from the start!'

'Really?' she croaked. When he set her back down on the ground, her knees were so weak that she clutched instinctively at Mal, who drew her back against the hard security of his body.

'I didn't realise you were so observant, Brett,' he said, and Copper wondered if the sarcastic edge was as obvious to Brett as it was to her.

Apparently not. Brett was nodding vigorously. 'I notice more than you think. You pretended to ignore each other but I could tell by the way you watched each other when you thought the other wasn't looking that it was real love!'

'What would you know about real love?' asked Mal, not even bothering to hide the edge to his voice this time.

'Not much,' his brother admitted. 'But I can recognise it when I see it all right, and I think you're both lucky.' The blue eyes sobered briefly. 'Very lucky,' he added seriously, and then grinned. 'Come on, let's celebrate!'

'I—' Copper was appalled to hear the squeak that came out when she opened her mouth, and cleared her throat in a desperate attempt to pull herself together. She couldn't stand here clutching Mal for ever. 'I'd better go and fetch Megan.' She tried again, not that she sounded much better second time around. But how could she be expected to sound normal when the world was still rocking around her and that wonderful, glorious, heart-stopping kiss was still strumming over her skin?

'I'll come with you,' said Mal easily.

'I'll go and make sure the beer's cold,' Brett offered. 'Don't be too long.'

'Let's hope everyone's as easy to convince as he is,' muttered Mal as his brother strode off towards the homestead. He looked down at Copper, who was leaning against him and trying to work up the determination to move away. 'Are you all right now?'

The concern in his voice snapped her upright. The last thing she wanted was for Mal to think that that kiss had meant any more to her than it had to him! 'I'm fine,' she said sharply, pushing her hair defensively behind her ears.

She set off down the track at a cracking pace, but as Mal refused to hurry, and she could hardly walk the whole way with him a ridiculous ten paces behind, she was forced to stop until he caught up and then carry on more slowly. The silence was agonising.

'Fancy Brett thinking we were in love all along!' said Copper at last, with a nervous laugh.

'Fancy,' Mal agreed expressionlessly, and she wished that she had kept her mouth shut.

The evening deepened as they walked back to the homestead with Megan. She skipped along between them, full of how naughty one of Naomi's toddlers had been and delighted to have been able to look down on his behaviour from the lofty heights of four and a half years. Copper was very aware of Mal, bending his head to listen gravely to his daughter's chatter. His gentleness with the little girl, somehow unexpected in such a strong, silent man, always wrenched at her heart. He must love

Megan very much if he was prepared to marry a woman he didn't love just for her sake.

The thought steadied Copper's nerves. The future might be an unknown quantity, her own feelings for Mal confused and uncertain, but for now it was enough to walk beside him through the hush of evening and smell the dryness of the gums drifting up from the creek.

Megan released their hands to run ahead, legs and arms completely uncoordinated. Stampeding up the steps, she disappeared into the kitchen and let the screen door clatter behind her.

'Are you going to tell her tonight?' Copper asked, worry beginning to seep back. Megan was used to having her father to herself; what if she was jealous?

'I may as well,' said Mal.

At the bottom of the verandah steps Copper faltered. The brief moment of serenity had dissolved, leaving her once more with all her doubts and uncertainties about the marriage and what it would mean. Once they had told Megan there would be no going back. They were going to walk up these steps and into a new life. For the next three years they would both be playing a part, deceiving everyone except each other.

'Do you really think we can carry it off?' she asked, abruptly apprehensive.

Mal had stopped beside her, and he turned now to look down into her troubled eyes. 'Of course we can,' he said, taking both her hands in a compelling clasp. 'I'll remember Megan and you remember your project, and we'll make it work together.' Strength seemed to flow through his hands, and Copper's fingers curled instinctively around his as she felt herself steadied.

They stood like that in the dusk, and the air between them shortened with a new intensity. Mal's grip on her hands tightened. 'It will be all right,' he promised quietly and slowly, very slowly, he bent his head and touched his lips to hers. The giddy excitement of before dissolved into tenderness and warmth and infinite reassurance, and Copper relaxed, leaning into his kiss for one enticing moment before Mal lifted his head.

Fingers entwined, they looked at each other in silence, as if dazzled by that unexpected glimpse of sweetness, and then Brett was banging through the screen door and calling to them to hurry up.

'Hey, break it up!' he ordered after one look at the tableau below him. 'You're not alone and the beer's getting warm!'

Inside, the kitchen seemed very bright, and Copper avoided Mal's eyes. She didn't know what to do with her hands. They felt very conspicuous, as if branded with the imprint of his fingers, and her lips tingled still with that brief, sweet kiss. Had he meant to kiss her? Had he been caught unawares, as she had, or had he just been trying to reassure her? Or had he heard Brett coming out from the kitchen and forced himself into his new role?

Megan was puzzled by the atmosphere until Mal took her on his knee and explained that he and Copper were going to be married so that Copper could stay with them all at Birraminda. 'Would you like that?'

Megan wasn't prepared to commit herself yet. 'How long will she stay?'

'A long time.'

The big blue eyes looked at Copper with unnerving directness. 'For ever?' she insisted, and Copper's smile went a little awry. Her eyes met Mal's for a fleeting moment over the small head.

'I hope so, Megan,' she said. By the time she left

Megan would be seven, nearly eight. That would seem like for ever to a child of four.

Megan seemed to take that as the end of the discussion. Copper had somehow envisioned the child rushing into her open arms, but Megan had seen too many strangers come and go to put her trust in anyone immediately. She simply slid off her father's knee and carried on with what she had been doing before, but when she was tucked up in bed, and Copper bent down to kiss her goodnight, two small arms shot up to cling around her neck.

'I love you,' said Megan fervently, and Copper's eyes stung with tears.

'I love you too, sweetheart.'

'I'm glad you're going to marry Dad,' she confided in a small voice.

'So am I,' whispered Copper, only to look up and see Mal watching them from the doorway.

'So is Dad,' he said.

'I can see him!' Megan tugged at Copper's hand, dancing up and down with excitement as she spotted Mal's lean, rangy figure appear through a door at the other side of the terminal, Brett close behind him. They paused for a moment, searching the crowd with their eyes.

Copper saw Mal at the same moment as Megan. Two weeks she and the child had been in Adelaide and now suddenly he was here, looking as quiet and as cool and as self-contained as ever, and all the careful composure that she had practised had crumbled at the mere sight of him. She wished she could be like Megan, running towards her father, confident in the knowledge that he would reach for her and smile and catch her up in his arms.

Pride forced Copper to follow more decorously, although her heart was hammering and her breathing uneven. 'Hello,' she said with a wavering smile as she reached them, and Mal stilled as he saw her at last.

She was wearing a summer dress in a faded yellow print, with a scoop neck and a soft swirl of skirt, and she was carrying a simple straw hat in her hands. Mal drew a long breath. 'Copper,' he said, and then stopped as if uncertain how to go on. His voice sounded odd, almost strained as they looked at each other.

Then he shifted Megan into one arm and reached slowly for Copper with the other, drawing her into his side, and she found herself lifting her face quite naturally for his kiss, her own arm creeping instinctively around his waist so that she could cling to him for the reassurance she hadn't even known she craved until then.

The touch of his mouth was electrifyingly brief. 'I've missed you,' he said as he raised his head.

Did he mean it, or was it just an act for Brett, who was watching them indulgently? 'I've missed you too,' she said huskily.

In her case it was true. She had brought Megan down to Adelaide over two weeks ago, and she had missed Mal more than she had thought possible. She had got used to him being there, used to the way he'd smile when he came in every evening. There had been times when she had almost forgotten that it was all a pretence.

Sometimes, when Mal had taken her riding along the creek, or when they'd sat on the verandah and watched the moon rise, it had seemed utterly natural that they should be together, talking easily about the day. It was only when their eyes had met unexpectedly that the tension would seep back into the atmosphere and Copper would remember that they weren't really in love. They were just pretending.

It wasn't as if Mal hadn't made his position absolutely clear. Judging by his ostentatious absence every night, Brett had no doubts about their relationship, but Copper had been all too conscious of the fact that she and Mal said a polite goodnight in the corridor and retired to their separate rooms.

'I suppose he thinks he's being tactful,' Mal had sighed that first evening, when Brett had taken himself off with much nodding and winking.

'You realise he's expecting us to fall into bed the moment the door closes behind him?' said Copper. She tried to sound amused but it didn't quite work.

'Of course he does.'

Copper fidgeted by the sink. 'Do you want…do you want to start now? Sharing a room, I mean,' she said awkwardly. 'Do you think it'll look odd if we don't?'

'Let Brett think we're making the most of it while he's out,' said Mal, unconcerned. 'It won't be long until we're married, and there'll be plenty of time for you to get used to sharing then.'

Copper should have felt relieved, but instead was left faintly disgruntled. In the face of such indifference she could hardly insist on dragging him to bed, could she?

During the day there was so much to do that it was easy to forget, but at night the knowledge that Mal didn't really want her was a constant reminder of the reality of the deal they had made, and as the weeks went by the contrast between the way things seemed and the way they were left Copper feeling increasingly edgy and irritable.

In the end, it was a relief when Mal flew her to Brisbane with Megan and put them on a plane to

Adelaide to organise the wedding, but being apart hadn't done anything to lessen the knot of mingled apprehension and anticipation inside her. It was permanently lodged somewhere in her stomach, and it tightened whenever she thought about Mal. As the prospect of marrying him drew nearer she grew more and more tense, until she felt hollow with nerves that looped and dived inside her. Now, in the busy airport building, she could feel them still, quivering distractingly just beneath her skin.

Things had been so busy at Birraminda that Mal and Brett had left it until now, two days before the wedding, before flying down in the small six-seater plane that sat on the landing strip. When they all flew back together afterwards, Copper would be Mal's wife. At the thought, a slow shiver snaked down her spine, and her shoulders flexed in response.

'Hey, Megan!' called Brett. 'Come and give me a hug so that Dad can say hello to Copper properly!'

Mal put his daughter down and she ran happily over to her uncle, who swung her up and tickled her until she squealed. Copper hardly heard. Mal had turned back to her, a smile lurking in the depths of his brown eyes, and the gentle trembling inside her erupted into a frantic flutter at the knowledge that he was going to kiss her again.

Only because Brett had reminded him that a brief touch of the lips wasn't enough for lovers who had been apart for two weeks, she told herself feverishly as Mal took both her hands and tugged her gently towards him. Her head struggled to hang onto the shreds of her pride and be the business-like Copper he expected her to be while her heart urged her to stop fighting the longing that unwound itself inside her. She had promised to act as if she was in love with him, instinct reasoned, and instinct won, allowing her to relax against Mal with a tiny sigh. It was only pretending, after all.

They were standing very close, marooned together in a hushed circle of awareness. The hustle and bustle of the airport faded into insignificance and there was only Mal, sliding his hands up her bare arms to her shoulders to cup her throat and tilt her face up to his. Very slowly he lowered his head, until his mouth was just brushing hers. Poised on the brink of release, Copper closed her eyes in delicious anticipation, and then the terrible, tantalising waiting was over. Mal secured her against him, his lips possessing hers in a kiss that was fierce and hard and yet achingly sweet.

Copper felt all her doubts dissolve in a golden rush of enchantment. Her hands crept up his chest and coiled around his neck as she abandoned herself to the swirl of sensation that carried her up out of time. It was bliss to feel his arms around her, to cling to the hard strength of his body and let the warmth of his mouth vanquish any last, lingering thoughts of resistance so utterly that when she sensed Mal begin to draw away, she couldn't prevent a murmur of protest. He stopped it with another kiss, softer this time and briefer, and then another, briefer still, until the green eyes opened languorously and Copper found herself back on earth.

Mal smiled at her dazzled expression. 'Hello,' he said, obedient to Brett's instructions.

'Dad, I've got a pink dress!' Megan tugged at his shirt, bored by the way they were just standing there looking at each other. She had much more exciting things to report.

Copper blinked and gave a rather shaky laugh, certain that she ought to be grateful for Megan's interruption. Take it lightly, she told herself frantically. It wasn't a real kiss. Mal had just been pretending because Brett was there. *She* had just been pretending too.

Hadn't she?

Her legs felt as if they belonged to another body entirely, and, acting or not, she was pathetically glad when Mal took her hand again. His clasp was calming, invigorating, indescribably reassuring.

'A *pink* dress?' he was saying to Megan, holding out his other hand to her. 'That sounds very smart.'

'Yes, and I've got a friend called Kathryn,' Megan informed him importantly. She skipped along beside them as Brett followed with the bags. 'I'm going to play with her this afternoon.'

'I hope you don't mind?' Copper moistened her lips, amazed to find that she sounded quite normal. 'I know you haven't seen Megan for a while, but she's had such a lovely time playing with my cousin's little girl.'

'No, I don't mind,' said Mal as they reached the car that Copper had borrowed from her father. 'I'm going to be taking Megan out tomorrow, while you and your mother do whatever it is women do before weddings, so I was hoping for a chance to get you on your own today.'

'Oh?' Hoping she didn't sound too pleased, Copper concentrated on digging into her bag for the car key.

Megan had run around the side of the car to pull on a doorhandle. Mal glanced back at Brett, who had been diverted by a pretty girl who wanted directions, and lowered his voice. 'I've arranged for a legal office here to draw up a contract for us,' he said, and Copper's fingers clenched around the key. 'Today will be our only chance to sign it before the wedding.'

'Fine,' said Copper in a tight voice, feeling a fool for allowing herself even a moment's dream that he might want to see her for herself. Well, what had she expected?

That one kiss would make any difference to Mal? He could hardly have found a better way of reminding her that their marriage was strictly business as far as he was concerned.

Megan chattered excitedly all the way back to the house and Copper was glad to concentrate on driving and on fighting down the wash of bitter disappointment. She was nervous, too, about Mal's first meeting with her mother, who had always been very fond of Glyn and who was less convinced than her father that Copper wasn't making a terrible mistake.

But she had forgotten how charming Mal could be when he tried. In a remarkably short space of time her mother was treating the two brothers like the sons she had never had, and by the time she had embarked on the most embarrassing stories from Copper's childhood Copper decided that she would prefer signing the contract after all.

Dan Copley, correctly interpreting her anguished glance, hastened to change the subject. 'I'm afraid that you're going to have to face a family party this evening, but we thought you and Caroline might like some time alone together this afternoon as you haven't seen each other for some time.'

'Sounds good to me,' said Mal. Glancing at his watch, he got to his feet. 'Brett and I are booked into a hotel in the city centre, so we'd better go and check in. Why don't you come with us, Copper, and I'll take you out to lunch?'

Copper smiled stiffly, knowing that as soon as he had got rid of Brett Mal would be whisking her off not to a romantic restaurant but to a lawyer's office, where they would sign three years of their lives away to a loveless marriage.

It didn't take long. Briefed by Mal from Birraminda, the admirably discreet lawyer had drawn up a concise document setting out exactly the terms of the cold-blooded deal they had agreed. Copper bent her head over the contract, pretending to read it through, but her eyes were shimmering with tears and when she signed her name it seemed to waver over the page.

'Here's your copy,' said Mal as they left. 'You'd better keep it safe.'

The day seemed hot and very bright after the air-conditioned cool of the office building, and Copper was glad of the excuse to hide her eyes with sunglasses. 'Can you keep mine until after the wedding?' she asked, rejoicing at the coolness in her voice. 'I don't want Mum or Dad finding it by mistake and knowing just what price I'm paying for our business to succeed.'

'If that's what you want.' Mal's face closed and he tucked the two contracts into his top pocket. 'Well, shall we go and have some lunch, since that's what we're supposed to be doing?'

They walked in strained silence down to the Torrens and along to a restaurant that overlooked the river, its tables shaded beneath a vine-covered pergola. Mal had changed at the hotel, and now, in light moleskin trousers and a pale blue washed cotton shirt, he looked casual and stylish and somehow unfamiliar. Copper had expected him to look out of place in the city, and it was oddly disconcerting to find him instead as at home in this cosmopolitan setting as he was riding Red under the huge outback sky.

Mal took the contracts out of his pocket and laid them on the table between them, where they lay taunting Copper in their pristine white envelopes. She tried not to look at them and fiddled with her fork as Mal dealt with the waiters, only lifting her head in surprise when he closed the wine list and coolly ordered a bottle of the best champagne.

'We *are* getting married the day after tomorrow,' he explained, in answer to her unspoken question.

'I know, but...well, we don't need to pretend when we're on our own, do we?' said Copper with some difficulty.

'No, but your parents might well ask you about your lunch, and I think they would expect us to have champagne, don't you?'

'I don't think they need any more convincing,' she said, concentrating on crumbling a roll between her fingers. 'Mum thought it was a bit sudden at first, but it helped that Dad had already met you, and he didn't seem to think there was anything odd about it at all. And they've both loved having Megan, so they feel as if you're part of the family already.' There were crumbs all over the tablecloth by now, and she brushed them into a careful pile. 'I don't think it's even occurred to them that we're not exactly what we're pretending to be.'

'Brett's the same,' said Mal. 'He's accepted the whole idea without question.'

Copper smiled painfully. 'We must be better actors than we think we are.'

There was a tiny pause. Was Mal remembering that kiss at the airport this morning? Or was he thinking of the contract, with its brisk specification that they should both behave in an appropriate manner whenever they were with other people?

'I suppose we must be,' he said at last.

The wine waiter was hovering, opening the champagne with a flourish. Copper could see the other diners smiling at the scene, obviously thinking that they were lovers, and she wanted to stand up and shout at them that it wasn't true, Mal didn't love her, it was all just for show and it meant nothing, *nothing*!

But she couldn't do that. She watched the bubbles fizzing in her glass and reminded herself about the successful business she would run and how happy her father was to know that his beloved project was going ahead. Her mind skittered to Mal, to the warmth of his mouth and the hardness of his hands, before she forced it back to the agreement they had made.

'Well…' She smiled bravely and lifted her glass. 'To our deal!'

Mal hesitated a moment, then touched his glass to hers. 'To our deal,' he said evenly.

There was a jarring silence as their eyes met and held, and then Copper managed to look away. She put her glass down on the white tablecloth rather unsteadily and tried desperately to think of something to say, but all she wanted to do was to snatch up those contracts lying there so mockingly and tear them into tiny pieces.

It was Mal who spoke first, anyway. 'So,' he said, 'how's it been going?'

'Not too badly.' Copper seized on the subject. Anything was better than that awful, jangling silence. 'I'm afraid the wedding's going to be bigger than we wanted, though. My mother's spent the last twenty-seven years looking forward to my wedding, and she's not going to be done out of it now.' She sighed. 'I kept telling her that we both wanted the ceremony to be simple, with just a quiet party afterwards, but every time I turn round she's invited someone else and the celebrations are getting more and more elaborate.'

'I'd have thought all the organisation would have appealed to someone with your business instincts,' said Mal indifferently. Nobody would guess that they were discussing his own wedding, Copper thought with a flash of resentment.

She turned the stem of her glass between her fingers. A couple were strolling along the riverbank opposite, hand in hand, absorbed in each other. Copper watched them with wistful green eyes. It had been a difficult two weeks. The strain of trying to keep her mother's plans under control had been bad enough, but far worse had been the effort of acting the part of the happiest girl in the world the whole time.

'I wouldn't have minded if it had been for a real wedding,' she said. 'But all the pretence gets tiring after a while, and it seems stupid to go to so much effort when you and I know the whole thing's just a charade.'

Mal's eyes were shuttered, expressionless. 'It'll soon be over,' was all he said.

'It won't be over for another three years,' said Copper bleakly, and he put down his glass.

'Are you trying to tell me that you're having second thoughts?'

She looked deliberately down at the contracts. 'It's too late for that now, isn't it? We've signed on the dotted line.'

'We're not married yet,' Mal pointed out impassively. 'It's not too late for you to change your mind.'

'And find somewhere else to set up the project? No.' Copper shook her head, avoiding his eye. How could she change her mind now, when her father was better, when Megan was thrilled at the prospect of being a bridesmaid? When cancelling the wedding would mean saying goodbye to Mal and never seeing Birraminda

again? She smoothed the cloth over the table. 'No, don't
take any notice of me. I'm just…'

'Nervous?' he suggested.

'Nervous?' she tried to scoff. 'Of course I'm not nervous!' She picked up her glass and made to drain it, only
to discover that it was empty. Feeling foolish, she set it
back on the table and tried to meet Mal's gaze confidently, but her defiance collapsed at one look from those
shrewd brown eyes. 'Oh, all right, I *am* nervous!' she
admitted crossly. 'If you must know, I'm absolutely terrified!'

'About the wedding?'

'About everything! We hardly know each other and
yet in two days' time we're going to be married.' She
flicked the white envelopes with her hand. 'It's all very
well to talk about contracts, but a piece of paper isn't
going to help us live together, is it?'

'At least you know what to expect out of the marriage,' said Mal, watching her over the rim of his glass.

'I know which jobs you'll expect me to do every day,
yes, but I don't know how we're going to get on, or
whether I'll be able to cope living in the outback, or
what it will be like suddenly becoming mother to a four-
year-old…or *anything*!' Copper finished despairingly.

'You've been living in the outback with Megan for
nearly two months,' said Mal reasonably. 'And as for us
getting on…well, we've got on in the past and I don't
see any reason why we shouldn't do the same again—
particularly as neither of us has any illusions about the
other or any false expectations about what the other one
really wants. And if it's a disaster at least you'll know
that you're not trapped and that your life isn't going to
change for ever. When three years is up, you'll have
established your new business. You'll be able to come

home to Adelaide, sit back and reap the benefits, and simply carry on as you were before.'

Copper tried to imagine walking away from Birraminda, from Megan, from Mal, and trying to pretend that they had never existed. She couldn't do it now. How would she be able to do it in three years' time? 'Somehow I don't think things will be the same,' she said sadly.

The first course arrived just then, immaculately presented on huge white plates, and as if at a signal the tension was broken. For the rest of the meal they kept the conversation carefully impersonal, and Copper was even able to relax slightly as she listened to the news from Birraminda and told Mal in her turn how excited Megan had been with everything she had seen and done.

It was only when they were drinking coffee that Mal brought the conversation back to their marriage. 'By the way,' he said casually, 'I've booked a hotel in the hills for Saturday night.'

Copper put her cup down into its saucer and looked at him blankly. 'What for?'

He raised an eyebrow. 'For our honeymoon, of course.'

'But...I thought we would be going straight back to Birraminda!'

'The wedding's not until five o'clock,' Mal pointed out patiently. 'By the time we get away it'll be much too late to fly back that night. We'll pick up Megan and Brett in the morning and go then. It's not a problem, is it?'

'No,' said Copper quickly. 'No, of course not.' Stupidly, she had never thought about a honeymoon. She had somehow assumed that they would spend their first night at Birraminda, where it would be so much easier to remember just why they were married. 'I just thought… Aren't you very busy at the moment?'

'One night isn't going to make much difference,' said Mal with a dry look.

It might not make a difference to him, but Copper knew that it was going to make a big difference to her! It was the night she was going to share a bed with Mal for the first time, the night she had to decide whether to lie stiffly by his side or to swallow her pride and succumb to the desire that seeped through her body whenever she thought about it. Copper had no idea whether she would ever find the courage to ask him to make love to her. Perhaps Mal would make things easy for her, she thought hopefully. He might take her in his arms and let passion sweep them up to a place where pride counted for nothing and no words were necessary…

Or he might get out his contract and check for the relevant clause, Copper amended with a bitter smile as she got dressed for the party that night. She was dreading the evening ahead. All the uncles and aunts and cousins and close family friends had been invited to meet Mal and Brett before the wedding, and she knew that she would have to spend the night being bright and cheerful and deliriously happy at the prospect of marrying a man who would expect her to put in a formal request before he would lay a finger on her!

The party was even worse than Copper had feared. Tense and jaded and headachy from too much champagne in the middle of the day, she had to endure endless teasing about her unsuitability for the outback. People kept kissing her and telling her what a lucky girl she was.

Copper's smile grew more and more brittle. Everyone seemed to be having a good time except her. Mal was relaxed and charming, unbothered by the fact that he was the centre of attention, while Brett had wasted no time at all in cornering her prettiest cousin and was meeting with plenty of encouragement. Her parents were delighted with their prospective son-in-law and all the relatives were entering into the party spirit with gusto.

That left Copper, inwardly cursing the day she had ever acquired a reputation for being good fun at any party. Why couldn't she have been so quiet and shy that nobody would notice if she sat in a corner by herself all evening? Better still, why couldn't she have been born without any family at all?

The party wore on and Copper's smile grew more desperate. She was listening to an elderly aunt tell her how fortunate she was to have found such a husband when she looked up to find Mal watching her from across the room. He was a still, steady focus in the hubbub, and all at once the thought of Birraminda hit Copper with the force of a blow.

The creek, the trees, the white blur of cockatoos wheeling in the sky and Mal, strong and sure beside her as the evening hush settled slowly around them... The longing to be there was so acute that Copper almost reeled. When someone stepped away and blocked Mal from sight, and she found herself back in the middle of the hot, noisy party, she felt almost sick with disappointment.

With disappointment and the heart-stopping realisation that she at least had no need to pretend. It was no use denying it any longer. She had fallen in love with him all over again.

CHAPTER SEVEN

WHY had it taken her so long to accept that she loved him? This time she couldn't tell herself that it was just a holiday romance, a passing passion for a stranger. This time it was for real.

Copper looked at her reflection in the long mirror. It was her wedding day. She was wearing a simple Twenties-style dress in ecru silk, with a drop waist, slender satin straps and a gossamer-fine top which whispered over her bare shoulders and floated ethereally with her slightest movement. Pearl drops trembled in her ears and there was frangipani in her hair. Her eyes were wide and dark and very green.

She ought to be happy. In a few minutes' time she would walk into the garden and marry the man she loved, surrounded by family and friends. She would be Mal's wife and he would take her back to Birraminda where she would have the challenge of setting up a project that would ensure her father's future and keep her busy and stimulated. What more could she want?

She wanted Mal to love her too. She wanted him to need her the way she needed him, to ache for her when she wasn't there, to feel that the world would stop turning without her.

But that hadn't been in the agreement, had it? Copper turned sadly away from the mirror and pulled the ribbon from her bouquet through her fingers as she remembered his words. 'I've had one wife who said that she loved me, and I don't want another.' Mal didn't want his life cluttered up with messy emotions. He wanted a practical wife, a business-like wife who would stick to the terms of the contract they had signed, and that was the kind of wife she would have to be.

'Dad's here!' Megan rushed in, trembling with excitement and still thrilled with the way the hairdresser had tied up her dusky curls with the palest pink ribbon to match her dress. 'Do you think he'll like my dress?'

'He'll think you're the prettiest little girl in the world,' Copper assured her, although her heart had started to do crazy somersaults and it was suddenly hard to breathe.

She hadn't been alone with Mal since that dreadful party. He had taken Megan out the next day while she had been swept into a whirl of activity by friends determined to celebrate her romantic marriage, and she had spent that evening quietly with her parents.

The knowledge of how much she loved him had held Copper in thrall for two days. She felt as if she were trapped in a strange dream-like state where she could walk and talk but everyone else was vaguely blurred. Nothing seemed real except her feelings for Mal, and now it was five o'clock and he was here and they were going to be married. Copper swallowed.

'You look beautiful.' Her father appeared behind her, turning her to hold her at arm's length so that he could admire her properly. 'This is the proudest day of my life,' he told her, his smile crooked with emotion. 'You're marrying a fine man, Caroline. We're going to miss you, but I know you'll be very happy together.'

Would they? Copper blinked back sudden tears. 'Thank you, Dad,' she said huskily, and kissed him on the cheek. 'Thank you for everything.'

Dan held her tightly for a moment, and then smiled

almost fiercely as he offered her his arm. 'Are you ready?'

'Are we ready, Megan?'

Megan nodded vigorously. She had been ready all day.

Copper drew a deep breath and took her father's arm. 'We're ready,' she said.

Together they walked through the house where Copper had grown up and out under the pergola at the back. The garden was decorated with white and gold balloons, and there were vases of yellow and white flowers on every table beneath wide white sunshades. Frangipani flowers floated in the pool and the air was sweet with their scent.

When Copper appeared, a hush fell over the guests grouped in a semi-circle around the celebrant, who stood with Mal and Brett, and they all turned to watch her walk across the grass. Copper noticed none of them. There was only Mal, waiting for her in a white dinner jacket that emphasised the darkness of his hair and the tanned, angular planes of his face, but which did nothing to detract from his distinctive air of quiet, tough assurance.

He turned too, as she approached, and as their eyes met Copper's world steadied miraculously. The dreamy haze that had enveloped her for the last two days snapped into focus and she was suddenly acutely aware of every detail: the gossamer touch of silk against her skin, the heady scent of the flowers in her hand, the feel of her father's arm and the concentration on Megan's face as she tried to remember her part.

And Mal, watching her with a smile that made her heart turn over.

Suddenly she was beside him. Her father squeezed her

hand, lifted it and kissed it before he stepped away, and Copper remembered to hand her flowers down to Megan, who peeped a smile at her as she took them very carefully. Then Mal was holding out his hand. She put hers into it and felt his fingers close around hers in a warm, strong clasp. Everything else ceased to exist.

Copper never knew how she got through the ceremony, but somehow she must have made the right responses in the right places, for Mal was sliding the ring onto her finger. She looked down at the gold band that linked her to him: they were married. Wonderingly, Copper lifted her eyes to his.

Mal's smile was oddly twisted as he looked down at her for a moment before cradling her face in his hands and bending his head very gently to kiss her. The touch of his mouth was enough to drench Copper in a golden, honeyed enchantment that spilled through her like a rush of light. The terms of the contract they had agreed, the watching crowd, the knowledge that Mal would never love her as she loved him, none of these mattered as their lips caught and clung and sweetness spun an invisible web around them, enclosing them in their own private world where time lost its meaning and a kiss could stretch into infinity and yet end much, much too soon.

A sentimental sigh gusted through the guests as Mal lifted his head and let Copper drift gently back to earth. Her eyes were still dark and dazed, but she managed a tremulous smile which seemed to be the signal for the garden to erupt into laughter and cheers.

Megan was clutching her flowers, wide-eyed and a little bewildered by the sudden noise. Copper crouched down to hug her and then lifted her up so that Mal could take her and hold her high and safe in his arms. Reassured that she was included in the magic that she had sensed between the two of them, Megan's face cleared, and she released her vice-like grip on her father's neck, smiling and ready to be let down so that she could run off and boast to her little friend about her part in the ceremony.

Copper's mother was weeping, and her father looked as if he had something hard and tight stuck in his throat. Copper just had time to kiss them both before she and Mal were surrounded and swamped in a tide of congratulations and kisses. At first Mal kept a tight, reassuring grip on her hand, but it wasn't long before they were separated and Copper was borne apart by friends who were meeting him for the first time and wanted to tell her how lucky she was.

'He's gorgeous!' they sighed enviously. 'And just right for you, Copper. It's all so romantic!' Then they would pause and add casually, 'His brother seems nice too. Is he married?'

Romantic was the one thing her marriage wasn't, Copper thought wistfully as she nodded and smiled and agreed that everything had worked out perfectly. Even seeing Glyn again wasn't enough to distract her from the gleam of gold on her finger that kept catching at the corner of her vision. I'm married, she kept telling herself disbelievingly. I'm Mal's wife.

Mal's housekeeper, she corrected herself sadly. 'To our deal,' Mal had toasted her, and the last, lingering enchantment of his kiss seeped away at the memory. A few kisses wouldn't change anything for Mal.

Unaware of the wistful look on her face as she hugged Glyn and turned away, Copper suddenly found Mal beside her. 'Come and dance,' he said, taking a possessive hold of her waist and drawing her over to the paved area under the pergola before anyone had a chance to intercept them with more congratulations.

It had grown dark as the party wore on and someone had lit the candle lanterns that were hung around the garden. They cast a flickering glow over Mal's face as he swung Copper into his arms. It was obvious that everyone had been waiting for them to start the dancing, for a suitably romantic song was playing and others soon joined them in the soft candlelight.

Mal's hand was warm and strong in the small of her back as he held her close, and Copper was overwhelmingly aware of him as she rested her head against his shoulder. To anyone else they must look as if they were madly in love, she thought. Out of the corner of her eye she could see the pulse beating in his throat, tantalisingly close. If she was a real bride, dancing with her new husband, she could turn her head and touch it with her lips. She could lift her face up to his and know that he would kiss her. She could whisper that she wished they were alone and let her pulse leap at the thought of the night to come.

But she wasn't a real bride, and she couldn't do any of the things she wanted to do. She could only lean a little closer and pretend that she was just acting, and wish that it could be true.

They were married. Copper succumbed to temptation and rested her face against Mal's throat, breathing in the clean, male scent of his skin. She felt boneless, weak with desire. Some time tonight they would say goodbye to everybody and drive up into the hills to the hotel and the door would shut behind them and they would be alone in their room. And what then? Would Mal really wait for her to ask before he touched her? Or would he take her hand and draw her down onto the bed and let the excitement that leapt between them whenever they kissed take its course? Copper's skin clenched at the thought and she shivered as anticipation beat a wild tattoo down her spine.

They danced in silence, holding each other like lovers. Copper was so absorbed in her dreams that it was a shock when Mal spoke at last. 'Who was that you were kissing?' he asked, as if the words had been wrenched out of him.

'Kissing?' Copper pulled slightly away, disorientated by the contrast between his cool voice and the intimacy of his hold. 'When?' she asked vaguely. Surely she had kissed everybody that evening?

'Just now.'

'Oh…' She made an effort to remember who she had been talking to before Mal had appeared at her side. 'That was Glyn.'

Mal's grip on her tightened almost painfully. '*Glyn*?' he echoed. 'Wasn't he the one who walked out on you? Who asked him to the wedding?'

'I did,' she said. 'Glyn was always a good friend. I couldn't not invite him.'

'I don't see why not,' said Mal disagreeably. 'I wouldn't have thought you'd have wanted to see him at all.'

'I don't hold any grudge against Glyn,' said Copper, a little puzzled by his attitude. If she hadn't known better, she might have thought Mal was jealous. 'If anything, we get on better now than we did before.'

It was true. The news of her engagement to Mal had dissolved the last vestiges of constraint between them and she had been able to talk to Glyn quite naturally as an old friend. And seeing him here tonight had made her realise just how differently she felt about Mal. Her relationship with Glyn had been warm and comfortable, but a tame thing compared to what she felt for the man who was holding her in his arms right now.

'You mean you've seen him before this evening?' Mal asked incredulously.

'A couple of times, yes.'

'And what about the so-called friend he left you for?' he went on in a harsh voice. 'Was she at those cosy reunions?'

Copper's face saddened, remembering how upset Glyn had been. 'No, Ellie's husband came back a couple of weeks ago, and Ellie feels that she owes it to him to give the marriage one last chance. So she and Glyn have agreed that they won't see each other for a while.'

'So he's free now,' Mal goaded her. 'You must be sorry you didn't wait for him a bit longer!'

He swung her round as he spoke. His arms were close around her, his head bent down to hers, for all the world a doting bridegroom. Sudden bitterness at the falsity of the picture sharpened Copper's tongue. 'I wouldn't have been able to set up business at Birraminda then, would I?' she said in a brief spurt of exasperation at his blindness. Couldn't he *see* how she felt? Wasn't it obvious whenever he kissed her?

She regretted the words as soon as they were spoken. The mention of business had been enough to harden Mal's expression, and it didn't take much to guess that he was thinking of his first wife who had also put business first.

'Reminding me of why you married me?' he asked, and Copper turned her face away into his shoulder.

'I don't think I need to do that,' she said in a low voice. Mal never forgot the real reasons for their marriage, and neither should she.

And yet, much later, when they finally managed to slip away from the party, Copper could think of nothing but the night to come. The tension of their exchange about Glyn had faded as the evening wore on, to be replaced by a new and very different kind of tension as the moment when they would be alone at last drew nearer.

The silence jangled between them as they drove through the wide, tree-lined streets and up into the hills, and Copper was gripped by such a strait-jacket of shyness that she would even have welcomed another argument to take her mind off the terrible, nameless longing that was drumming through her.

Mal was an overwhelming figure beside her in the darkness. Copper tried not to look at him, but her eyes kept flickering back to his profile, to the unyielding line of his jaw and the way the faint greenish light from the dashboard glanced over his lips. Every time her gaze fell on his mouth the knot of nerves would twist painfully inside her, and she would jerk her eyes away with a suppressed gasp, only to find herself staring at the strong, competent hands on the steering wheel and remembering how they had once felt against her body instead. It was all too easy to forget just why she had married him when desire tightened like a mesh over her skin.

By the time they reached the hotel Copper was vibrating with awareness, and her throat was so tight that she could hardly speak. It was Mal who checked in, Mal who replied to the hotel manager's discreet congratulations and Mal who closed the door to their room at last, leaving Copper standing nervelessly in the middle of the carpet.

'Thank God that's over,' he sighed, dropping into one

of the armchairs and wrenching at his bow tie until it dangled around his neck.

'Yes,' was all she could manage. She watched as Mal undid the top button of his shirt and closed his eyes, leaning his head back against the chair and pushing his hands through his dark hair. Her breath shortened.

'It went all right, though, didn't it?'

'Yes,' she said on a gasp.

He looked tired. She wanted to go over to him, to stand behind him and massage his shoulders, to lean down and drop tiny kisses over his face until he smiled and forgot his exhaustion. The longing was so acute that Copper's bones dissolved. Her legs gave way abruptly and she collapsed onto the edge of the chair opposite his.

There was something hard and tight inside her, strangling the air in her lungs and making her heart boom and thud in her ears. Copper forced herself to concentrate on breathing. Inflate the lungs, hold it a moment, breathe out. It was easy when you tried.

Then Mal opened his eyes without warning and all her effort was wasted as the air evaporated around her, leaving her stranded, suspended in mid-breath, unable to speak or move or even think. The deep brown gaze held her transfixed for what seemed like an eternity before Copper was able to stumble to her feet with a cross between a gasp and a gulp. 'I—I think I'll have a shower,' she stammered, and fled to the bathroom.

Her body pounded as she stood under the shower and images from the past slid over her, as physical as the streaming water but infinitely more disturbing. She wanted to coil herself around him, just as she had done before. She wanted to kiss his throat and taste his skin and listen to his heart beating. She wanted to spread her hands over his back and glory in the hardness of his body.

Copper's hands were shaking as she wrapped a towelling robe around her, and when she looked in the mirror her eyes were a bright, almost feverish green. Her skin felt as if it were pulsating with a life of its own, twitching and rippling and aching for Mal and the way things had once been between them.

'All you have to do is ask...' Mal's words reverberated down her spine and Copper welcomed the suddenly invigorating surge of anger that accompanied the memory. It wasn't fair of him to make her beg him to make love to her. What did he expect her to say? Oh, by the way, Mal, I would like to sleep with you after all?

Copper stared at her reflection. She couldn't do it...could she?

Mal had been quite straightforward, after all. He hadn't seen any reason why they shouldn't have a satisfying physical relationship. The only thing he didn't want was to get emotionally involved, but she didn't have to tell him that she was in love with him. Surely anything would be better than spending three years racked by this terrible yearning?

'Have you fallen asleep in there?'

Copper started as Mal's shout broke through her fevered speculation. 'No, no...I'm just coming.' Drawing a deep breath, she tied her robe more securely. It was now or never.

When she opened the door, Mal was sitting barechested on the side of the bed, taking off his shoes and socks. 'I was beginning to wonder if you were planning to spend the night in there,' he said, without looking up.

'Sorry.' Copper's voice came out as a pathetic squeak. This was the moment. All she had to do was cross the room and sit down next to him. All she had to do was lay her hand on the warm, bare skin of his back. Make love to me, Mal—that was all she had to say. It wouldn't be so hard, she told herself. But her feet wouldn't move and the words stuck in her throat, and then Mal was standing up and heading for the bathroom in his turn and the moment had passed.

Sick with disappointment and despising herself for her lack of courage, Copper pushed open the door onto the balcony and let the night air cool her burning cheeks. Far below her she could see the lights of Adelaide, strung in spangled lines across the plain between the hills and the sea. Somewhere down there amongst them all her family and friends were still celebrating her marriage, perhaps imagining her up here with Mal, blissfully happy, in love, confidently facing a lifetime together instead of three years of tension and frustration.

'What are you doing out there?' Mal stopped as he came out of the bathroom and saw Copper still standing on the balcony, barefoot and half hidden in the shadows. After a moment's hesitation he stepped out onto the balcony as well, and leant on the rail a couple of feet away from her. He had taken off his trousers and was wearing only his boxer shorts, and his body was lean and powerful and tantalisingly close.

'I was thinking,' Copper answered him at last. A light breeze rustled through the trees and lifted her hair. She clutched the robe at her throat with both hands, as if she were cold.

'What about?'

'Oh…just that this isn't what I imagined my wedding night would be like,' she said, keeping her eyes firmly on the city lights below.

'What did you imagine?' asked Mal quietly from the shadows, and Copper swallowed.

'A room like this, perhaps,' she said painfully. 'A view like this. A night like this. I thought it might be all these things but I never thought that everything else would be so different.'

'I saw the way you looked when you were talking to Glyn this evening.' Mal's voice was flat, rather harsh. 'I suppose you imagined you would be with him.'

Copper clutched her robe tighter. 'I just imagined that I would be with someone I loved, with someone who loved me,' she said with difficulty. 'That's all.'

There was a long, airless silence. Copper was excruciatingly aware of the beat of her own heart, of the soft towelling next to her skin, of Mal's powerful frame and the unbearable gap between them.

'Mal?' she said, suddenly urgent.

'Yes?'

'I—I know it's not like that for us, but...' Copper's voice petered out in despair as her nerve began to fail. 'But I've been thinking about what you said...' she struggled on desperately, before she lost it altogether.

She felt rather than saw Mal straighten, suddenly alert. 'What did I say?' he asked softly.

'You—you said that you wouldn't touch me unless I asked you to,' said Copper in a rush. She was still staring down at the distant lights that winked and glimmered as if mocking her stammered attempts to explain. 'And...and I wondered if...well, if we could pretend— just for tonight—that...that it was all how I'd imagined it after all, and that we'd just got married be- cause...because we loved each other and not because of some deal we've made?'

She trailed off, unable to look at Mal but miserably

aware of his silence. 'I mean…you don't have to. It's probably not a good idea, anyway,' she said desperately. 'It's been a long day and we're both tired and—'

The rest of the sentence died in her throat as Mal closed the gap between them and very gently turned her towards him. 'I'm not tired,' he said softly, sliding his hand around her throat to tilt her face with his thumb so that she had to meet his eyes. 'Are you?'

Copper's heart stopped at the expression in his eyes. 'N-no,' she whispered.

'Shall we pretend, then?' Mal's thumb was drifting along her jaw, feathering down her throat, the merest graze of his fingers enough to send sparks fizzling through her veins.

'J-just for tonight,' stammered Copper. It was suddenly terribly important that Mal didn't think that she was changing the rules already. Let him believe that she was just regretting what might have been instead of feeling weak with need for him. Let him think anything as long as he kissed her soon.

'Just for tonight,' Mal confirmed gravely, but there was a smile gleaming at the back of his eyes and his hand was sliding around to stroke the nape of her neck. 'How shall we begin?'

The caress of his fingers sent tiny shudders of desire down Copper's spine, and all at once it was easy. 'We-ell…' She pretended to consider. 'If I were in love with you, I wouldn't be at all shy. I might step a bit closer—like this,' she said, lifting her hands to his chest and spreading them over his bare skin with a wonderful sense of release. 'And then I *might* kiss you—just here.' She touched her lips tantalisingly to the pulse in his throat before kissing her way slowly, deliciously, up to the angle of his jaw and then the lobe of his ear. 'Or maybe here,' she whispered as she went. 'Or here…or here…'

Mal had stilled at her first touch, but as her kisses grew more provocative he tangled his fingers in the softness of her hair and tipped her head back almost fiercely. 'If *I* were in love with you,' he said, looking down into her face, 'I'd tell you that you looked beautiful today.' His voice was deep and very low. 'I'd tell you what it felt like to watch you and know that you were mine at last.' Slowly, very slowly, he lowered his head until his lips were just brushing hers. 'I might even tell you that I'd spent all day thinking about this,' he murmured, and then the waiting was over and his mouth came down on hers.

Copper's mouth opened like a flower to the sun. Her arms slid up to his shoulders and locked around his neck as she kissed him back, giddy with the pleasure of being able to touch him and taste him, of knowing that he was real and that whatever happened tomorrow, tonight was theirs.

Mal had released her head only to gather her hard against him, his hands insistent through the towelling robe, and Copper gasped with excitement as his lips left hers. 'I *think*,' he murmured wickedly against her throat, 'we would make ourselves more comfortable, don't you? If we were in love, that is,' he added, brushing the robe apart to tease kisses along her shoulder.

'I'm sure we would,' she said unsteadily.

Inside, Mal switched off the overhead light, and for a long moment they just looked at each other in the warm glow cast by the bedside lamps, both held by the knowledge of what was to come. Copper's body strummed with anticipation as Mal took off his boxer shorts and then, very deliberately, reached out at last and loosened the belt of her robe so that he could slide the towelling off her shoulders and down her arms until it fell in a soft heap at her feet.

Her skin was luminous in the soft light and Mal drew an uneven breath, his hands unsteady as they spanned her waist. 'Copper,' was all he said, but he made her name a caress, and Copper's every sense snarled at the desire in his voice and the expression in his eyes and the hard promise of his hands. Not daring to breathe in case she broke the spell and woke to find that this was all a dream, Copper waited, poised breathless on the brink, and then Mal smiled and secured her against him as he drew her down onto the soft bed, and the world shattered into a thousand spinning fragments of delight.

The thrill of skin meeting skin was so intense that Copper gave something between a gasp and a sob. Her hands were impatient over him, exploring the texture of taut flesh over muscles, loving his sleekness and his strength as her body clamoured for his possession, but Mal was in no hurry.

He stretched her beside him and swept his hand luxuriously up from the gentle curve of her hip. 'If we were in love,' he whispered as he reached her breast, 'I'd tell you that I'd dreamed about you, about touching you like this...' His fingers circled and teased, searing Copper's senses until she arched beneath him, and when he bent his head to allow his lips to follow their scorching progress she could only sob his name, afire with a nameless, electrifying hunger.

He explored every inch of her without haste, lingering possessively over each bewitching curve, treasuring each dip and hollow, ravishing, exploring, smiling against her skin. Mal's hands were as slow and sure as Copper remembered, his mouth as enticing, but her need for him was greater, much greater than before. His body was like tempered steel, unyielding and yet warm and supple and gloriously exciting.

Intoxicated by it, she tumbled over him, running her hands down his flank and trailing kisses from his chest down to his flat stomach, tickling him with her tongue and her tousled hair until Mal groaned and swung her back roughly beneath him. He punished her with long, slow kisses, deliberately prolonging her torment, and it was only when Copper begged for release, her words tumbling incoherently over each other, that he gave himself up to the urgency that was spiralling out of control.

Copper cried out at the feel of him inside her. Wrapping herself around him, she sobbed his name, and Mal responded instinctively to her unspoken appeal, taking her with him through the wild, clamorous, spinning hunger until the insistent plunging rhythm of their bodies bore them out of it and onto the edge of eternity.

There they paused for one dazzling, timeless moment before a great, unstoppable surge of feeling broke over them, sweeping them out over the abyss, swirling them onwards and upwards and onwards again. Awed, abandoned, Mal and Copper clung together, calling each other's names for reassurance, and then, just when it seemed that they would shatter like glass, they exploded into sheer ecstasy that blotted out anything but each other and let them spiral slowly downwards through the afterglow at last.

Aeons later, Copper opened her eyes languorously and was amazed to find that the room was still there, looking quite unchanged. They had left the door to the balcony open and the breeze was billowing the curtains but otherwise all was still, as if time itself had stopped. She could hear the sound of their ragged breathing, but it seemed to come from a long way away. Copper's real self seemed to be still spinning through the stars and she felt curiously disembodied, able to look down on herself lying tangled with Mal in drowsy limbo.

She lay contentedly, her hands smoothing lovingly over his back, savouring the warm, compact body lying relaxed and heavy on hers, and listened to their breathing as it slowed and steadied. Mal stirred then and lifted himself up slightly to smile down at Copper and smooth the hair tenderly away from her face.

'I know we're pretending,' he said very softly, 'but if I was in love with you, I would tell you how much I loved you now.'

The truth trembled on Copper's tongue but she held it back. If she told him that she was really in love with him he might feel irritated or embarrassed, or feel that she expected him to say it back, and she wanted nothing to spoil this magical night. Instead she wound her arms around his neck and pulled his head down to blot out reality with a kiss.

'And I would say I loved you too.'

CHAPTER EIGHT

WHEN Copper woke the next morning, Mal was already up and dressed. He was standing by the dressing table, but as she stirred he looked across at her. Her hair was tumbled, her eyes green and sleepy, her mouth dreamily curved as she stretched languidly, and something blazed in his eyes before the old guarded look clanged back into place.

Only half-awake, but instinctively sensing the change in him, Copper pulled herself up onto the pillows and clutched the sheet over her breasts. 'Good morning,' she said, ridiculously shy after all they had shared the night before.

'Good morning.' Mal was pleasant but distant, as if he had withdrawn behind some invisible barrier.

Copper's throat tightened. What had happened? Last night he had made love to her with a passion that was beyond words. How could he be standing there now, looking so cool, so quiet, so utterly unreachable? Then her gaze dropped and she saw what he was holding in his hands.

The contract.

Mal dropped it onto the dressing table, where it landed with a faint slap. 'That's your copy,' he said, his face blank of all expression. 'You'd better keep it safe.'

The last lingering traces of enchantment cracked and splintered, falling in icy shards around Copper and leaving her cold and bereft. He could hardly have made it clearer that last night had indeed been a pretence as far

132

as he was concerned. She turned her face away on the pillow. 'I will,' she said dully.

She was silent and strained as they drove back down the winding road to the city to pick up Megan. The whole day had taken on a nightmarish atmosphere. Over breakfast Mal had behaved as if absolutely nothing had happened between them. He'd talked about taking the opportunity to stock up on fresh fruit and vegetables and about what time he had arranged to meet Brett at the hotel for the return trip, but he'd said nothing at all about the long, sweet hours they had held each other in the darkness.

She had asked him to pretend to be in love with her, and he had pretended. That was all there was to it.

Copper clung to the thought of the night to come. The contract belonged to the harsh light of day, but surely once darkness fell, and they closed the bedroom door, they could recreate the tenderness and joy once more. She wouldn't even mind that Mal was pretending, Copper told herself, as long as he would take her in his arms again.

She longed to be back at Birraminda, but the day seemed perversely long. Stores had to be bought, Megan had to be picked up, goodbyes had to be said, and then Brett was late meeting them at the hotel so they had to hang around for over an hour before he turned up.

It was a long flight back to Birraminda in the tiny plane. Everyone was tired and on edge. Mal scowled at the controls, Brett was sullen and Megan fractious, and Copper just wanted to shut herself in a dark room and be left alone to enjoy a good cry.

When they touched down on the rough landing strip it was nearly dark, and they still had to pack the fruit and vegetables and everything else Copper had brought with her into the pick-up truck and then out again at the homestead. Megan had to be fed and bathed and put to bed, but she was over-tired and over-excited after all the attention of the last couple of weeks and the whole process culminated in a shattering tantrum. Copper just wished that she could do the same. Her head was aching and her eyes felt gritty with unshed tears.

By the time she and Mal were able to go to bed, the night before seemed like a lifetime ago and Copper was too tired even to think about the plans she had made to rediscover the sense of magic they had shared. 'I'm exhausted!' she sighed, sinking down onto the edge of the bed as Mal closed the door.

'There's no need to start dropping hints,' he snarled, and she stared at him, surprised out of her lethargy.

'What do you mean?'

Irritably, Mal began to strip off his shirt. 'I mean you don't have to think up an excuse every night to avoid sleeping with me. You made yourself clear enough last night.'

'But…but I wasn't hinting,' stammered Copper. 'I was just saying that I was tired!'

'Fine,' said Mal, chucking his shirt onto the back of a chair and reaching for a towel. 'You're tired, I'm tired, so let's just get some sleep.'

When he came back from the bathroom, Copper was lying stiffly under the sheet with her back turned to the light. Her eyes were squeezed shut and she was pretending to be asleep, but she was vibrating with awareness. She could sense Mal moving around the room, hear the clunk of his boots hitting the floor and the sound of the zip as he undid his trousers, and she could picture him so clearly that she might as well have had her eyes wide open.

Then he clicked off the light and the bed dipped as he got in beside her. Copper held her breath in the sudden darkness. If he turned to her now, if he spoke, everything might still be all right. She would meet him halfway and burrow into the comfort of his arms and they would laugh together over the tensions and misunderstandings of the day.

But Mal didn't turn. He didn't even say goodnight. He simply settled himself down and went calmly to sleep.

Aching with disappointment, Copper edged onto her back. Had he just been indulging her the night before? The thought made her burn with humiliation. If Mal thought she was going to beg him to make love to her every night, he had another think coming. She had asked once, and she was damned if she was going to ask again! He could make the first move next time.

In the dark hours of the morning Copper came to a decision. It was easy to make angry resolutions, but it didn't change the fact that she still loved him. Somehow she was just going to have to make him fall in love with her as well. If Mal wanted a practical, unromantic wife, that was the kind of wife she would be. She would play her part and she wouldn't ask anything of him, and perhaps, in time, he would realise that she was nothing like Lisa and decide that he wanted a wife who loved him after all.

Over the next few weeks, Copper worked really hard at being what Mal wanted her to be. Most of her time she spent with Megan, starting her on elementary lessons with the books that she had bought in Adelaide. She gave Megan the security of knowing that she would be firmly disciplined if she was naughty, comforted if she was hurt and loved whatever happened.

When she wasn't with Megan, Copper cleaned and tidied and scrubbed and polished, and gradually the homestead lost the faintly neglected air it had worn when she arrived. She sorted out the storerooms and reorganised the office and even offered to help Mal with all the paperwork. There was the camp site to be established too. Copper threw herself into the project, setting aside time every day to study tenders for the construction work or redraft their plans in the light of everything that she was learning about real life in the outback.

She was so busy that it was easy to get through the days, but the nights were much harder. It wasn't too difficult to talk normally together during the day, but every night when they went to bed they lay carefully apart and didn't talk at all. Copper made no demands on Mal, but as it became obvious that her careful strategy wasn't working she became increasingly crotchety and frustrated.

She was trying her best to be a good outback wife but it obviously wasn't enough. She couldn't brand a cow or ride a horse very well, and nothing else seemed to count with Mal. She got no credit for keeping the house or noticing that one of the jackaroos wasn't feeling well or discovering that Naomi was deeply unhappy. What thanks did she get for caring for his daughter and ensuring that they all got three square meals a day? None!

The more Copper brooded, the more her resentment grew—until she had almost convinced herself that she wasn't really in love with Mal at all. How could she be in love with a man who barely acknowledged her existence?

As the weeks passed, so the tension grew, until it shimmered like the heat haze over the scrub and the air between them twanged and whined, and finally snapped.

She was in the office one day, working on some figures, when Mal strode in and informed her that the men
would need sandwiches for lunch as he was sending
them out to check the fences.

Copper laid down her pen, a dangerous look in her
green eyes. 'Why didn't you tell me this at breakfast?'

'I didn't know at breakfast,' said Mal, with a touch
of impatience. 'I thought it would take them most of the
day to finish off what they started yesterday, but they've
made good time and it's worth them making a start on
those fences this morning.'

'If they're making such good time, they can make
their own sandwiches,' said Copper, and picked up her
pen again.

There was an ominous silence. 'Why can't you make
them?' asked Mal in a glacial voice.

'Because I'm busy,' she snapped, and her lip curled
dismissively.

'You're not busy; you're just playing around with that
precious project of yours!'

Copper looked up furiously. 'I am not *playing around*!
I'm working out the cheapest way to bring in supplies
for the tour groups and how we can calculate that into
our costs. I think that's a bit more important than making
a few sandwiches that you are all more than capable of
making yourselves!'

'Of course, you would think that was more important,'
said Mal contemptuously. 'You're obsessed with your
business. You're always in here, fussing over your files.
The rest of Birraminda could fall to pieces as far as
you're concerned, as long as your camp site survives to
keep your business going!'

'Do you want to know what I've done so far this
morning, Mal?' said Copper, hanging onto the shreds of

her temper with difficulty. 'I've cooked breakfast for you and your men, I've washed your dishes afterwards and put everything away, and I've swept your floor and cleaned your units. I've made your bed and washed your clothes and scrubbed out your shower.

'And in the middle of it all,' she swept on, without giving Mal a chance to speak, 'I've fed your dogs and your hens and made a meatloaf for your lunch and two apple pies for your dinner, not to mention some ice-cream for the freezer. I've washed and dressed your daughter and kept her entertained, and now that I've got a few minutes to myself, I'm working out how to run a profitable business that will bring some much needed cash into your property, judging by your accounts—which I have also kept up to date. And you *dare* to suggest that I don't do anything for Birraminda!'

'I'm not accusing you of sitting around all day,' said Mal, unmoved by her tirade. 'But you're only doing what any housekeeper would do, and you knew exactly what you were taking on when you signed that contract.'

'I didn't realise that I was signing up to three years' slavery!' she said bitterly.

'If you've got so much to do, why did you take over the evening cooking for the men?' he demanded. 'Naomi was perfectly happy doing it.'

'Naomi was *not* happy doing it!' Copper flared. 'If you had eyes to see anything beyond your stupid cows, you'd know that.' Pushing back her chair, she walked edgily over to the window, clutching her arms together defensively. 'I found Naomi in tears one day,' she said, swinging round to face Mal accusingly once more. 'She's got two small children and another one on the way, Bill's out all day, and she can't cope with the cooking on top of everything else. When I spoke to her she was so miserable that she was ready to take the children and go back to her mother in Brisbane. If I hadn't listened to her and tried to make her life a little easier, by taking over the cooking and looking after the children when I can, she'd be there now.'

Copper paused angrily, then swept on. 'Bill's not a demonstrative type, but anyone can see that he adores his wife, and if she'd gone he'd have followed her, and you'd have been left short of a man. And since you've spent the last few weeks telling me how busy you are, I assumed that you would prefer it if I could persuade Naomi to stay. But are you grateful?' She flung her arms out in a furious gesture. 'No! You think you can just walk in here and snap your fingers and I'll drop everything to make a few sandwiches. And when I object, you start quoting the terms of the contract to me!

'Well, I'm a good businesswoman, Mal,' she went on, green eyes flashing, 'and I read that contract before I signed it. There was nothing in it about making sandwiches on your say-so. What there *was* was an agreement that I would spend part of my time setting up the project which was the only reason I married you in the first place, in case you've forgotten!'

'I hadn't forgotten,' said Mal icily. There was a white look about his mouth and he was as angry as she was. 'You never give me a chance to forget.'

'That's good coming from you!' Copper retorted, too angry now to care what she said. 'You hardly ever open your mouth except to quote that agreement at me! If you had your way I'd spend all day at your beck and call. Perhaps I should be grateful you let me sleep at night?'

'There's no question about you doing anything else at night, is there?' he said savagely, and turned on his heel. 'You're not as essential as you think you are, Copper.

We managed perfectly well before you came, and we'll manage again whether you're here or not.' He paused with his hand on the door and looked back at where she stood, rigid with temper, by the window. 'I'll make the sandwiches myself—I wouldn't want to drag you away from your important business!'

The door slammed behind him and Copper was left alone to grind her teeth and find the only outlet for her feelings in throwing a stapler across the room to where Mal had been. She had worked her fingers to the bone for him and all he could do was quote the contract at her and demand sandwiches! How had she ever thought she was in love with him? He was arrogant, selfish and a bully, and she hated him!

Too angry to sit still, Copper paced around the office. So Mal thought she was obsessed with business, did he? He hadn't seen anything yet! All that was left to her out of the whole wretched business of her marriage was the chance to create a superlative new tourist location. Copper vowed to prove to Mal that ''playing around'' would produce the best tours in the country! She would show him just how obsessive she could be!

The atmosphere that evening was tight-lipped. Copper talked exclusively to Brett and was careful to say nothing that was not in some way concerned with the project. Mal himself hardly said a word, except to announce that he was flying to Brisbane the next morning and wouldn't be back until the following day.

Copper told herself that she was glad to see him go, and was furious with herself for listening for his step on the verandah all day, or noticing how empty the doorway seemed without him. That evening she and Brett sat in the creaky wicker chairs and drank a beer together, and the very air seemed to echo with Mal's absence.

Brett glanced at her shadowed face. 'Have you and Mal had an argument?'

'What makes you think that?' said Copper, not without some sarcasm. It must have been obvious that she and Mal were hardly talking to each other.

'Mal walked around looking like a thundercloud all yesterday and when I showed a bit of brotherly concern, and asked what was the matter, he bit my head off,' said Brett ruefully. 'Talk about bears and sore heads!'

It was no use pretending that nothing was wrong, Copper thought, and it wasn't as if real couples never had arguments. 'If you must know, he's being impossible!' she confided, and was comforted to find Brett such a sympathetic listener.

'I know,' he said with feeling. 'I've been doing my best to avoid him for weeks! I'm not saying he isn't a great bloke, but when he's like that the only thing to do is take cover. You should have heard him when I forgot to check the jackaroos had finished the fencing the other day! He tore me into little pieces and threw me all over the paddock.'

Brett grimaced at the recollection and then shrugged it off. 'If you think it's hard being his wife, you should try being his brother sometimes,' he said. 'At least he's in love with you.'

'Is he?' Copper was unable to prevent the bitter note in her voice. She couldn't tell Brett the truth about her relationship with Mal, but she didn't see why she should pretend that it was roses all the way either. 'You'd never have guessed it if you'd heard him yesterday.'

'He's not very good at showing his feelings, that's all.' Brett shifted a little uncomfortably in his chair. 'I haven't said anything before, but he had a bad time with Lisa. I hated her,' he said with sudden vehemence. 'She was the most beautiful woman I've ever seen, but she destroyed something in Mal. She made him hard and bitter and he was never the same again.'

Brett sighed and shook his head as he took a pull of his beer. 'That's why I was so glad when he married you—apart from my own bitter disappointment, of course!' he interposed with a grin. 'You're good for him, Copper. He shut himself off for too long, as if he didn't have any emotions at all. It's a good sign that he can get angry again.'

'I'll remember that the next time we have an argument,' said Copper with a rather twisted smile, and Brett put his beer down on the verandah.

'Tell you what, let's have a bottle of wine with our meal tonight,' he suggested. 'We deserve a treat. Mal's snug in some hotel, so the least we can do is show that we can have a good time without him!'

In the end they had two bottles, and Copper felt decidedly fragile the next day. There was no word from Mal as to when he would be back, and when Brett came in that evening, also very much the worse for wear, she asked if she ought to ring the hotel and find out what had happened to him. 'Do you think he's all right?' she said, despising the anxious note in her voice.

'Of course he is,' said Brett. 'He must have decided to stay another night, that's all.'

'Wouldn't he have let me know?'

'Perhaps he forgot,' Brett said casually, sinking down onto a chair and clutching his head. 'God, I feel awful!'

Copper ignored the state of his head. Mal would come back when he was good and ready, and not before, but it wouldn't kill him to let her know when to expect him, would it? He had probably written into his wretched contract that she was to wait dutifully and be prepared to serve him a meal whenever he deigned to appear!

She banged the oven door shut crossly and went to sit down at the kitchen table next to Brett. 'Do you think another bottle of wine would make us feel better?' he said.

'Would Mal approve?' she asked, and he grinned.

'No.'

Copper smiled brilliantly back at him. 'In that case, I'll get the corkscrew!'

They had just started on their first glass when they heard the sound of the plane overhead, and they exchanged glances of ludicrous dismay. 'Hadn't you better go and meet him?' she suggested, but Brett said that he was feeling brave.

'He's got the pick-up truck at the landing strip,' he pointed out. 'Let's brazen it out!'

'You're right.' Copper straightened her shoulders. 'There's no reason why we shouldn't have some wine if we feel like it, is there?'

'Absolutely not.'

The situation was so ridiculous that they both began to giggle nervously like naughty children, egging each other on with their bravado. When Mal walked in, it was to find his wife and his brother sitting at the kitchen table, convulsed with laughter.

Copper's giggles stuck in her throat as soon as she saw Mal, and her heart constricted inexplicably. Her first impulse was to throw herself into his arms and beg him not to go away and leave her again, but somehow she forced her voice to a nonchalance she was far from feeling. *She* wasn't the one who had swanned off to the city without bothering to let anyone know when she would return, was she?

'Oh, you're back.'

'Yes, I'm back.' Mal looked grimly from one to the other. 'What do you two think you're doing?'

'We've been consoling each other for your absence,' said Copper acidly.

'Well, I didn't mind you not being here,' Brett put in, 'but I thought it was my duty to comfort Copper.'

'It doesn't look to me as if she's in much need of comfort,' Mal bit out. 'If I'd known you were going to be like this, I would have come back on my own.'

'What do you mean?' she said, puzzled. 'You are on your own.'

'No, I'm not. I've brought you a housekeeper. Although I don't think she's going to be very impressed when she sees what kind of state you get into as soon as I leave you alone!'

Copper exchanged a baffled glance with Brett. 'You've brought a *what*?' she said stupidly.

'A housekeeper,' Mal confirmed, and then turned at the light step on the verandah outside. 'Here she is now.'

Even as he spoke a very slender, very neat girl with honey-coloured hair and intensely blue eyes stepped into the kitchen and smiled at Brett and Copper, who were staring at her, slack-jawed with surprise. 'Hi,' she said.

'This is Georgia,' said Mal.

Copper could hardly wait for Mal to close the bedroom door before she rounded on him. 'How dare you bring that girl here without consulting me?' she stormed. 'I thought you were going to Brisbane on business?'

Mal's jaw tightened ominously. 'I was.'

'And you just happened to find a pretty girl to bring home with you, is that it?'

'I explained all this when I introduced Georgia,' he

said impatiently. 'I had to go and see our accountant, who's an old friend. He told me about a friend of his daughter's who was looking for a job in the outback and asked me if I knew of anyone who might need someone.'

'So you said you did?' said Copper with a withering look, and he clenched his teeth, keeping his temper with difficulty.

'No, I said *you* did. You were the one who was complaining that you had too much to do. It seemed a good opportunity to find a girl to help you, if only to prevent any more accusations of treating you like a slave! And Georgia's an outback girl. She should be really useful.'

'Oh, yes, she's ideal,' said Copper jealously.

Over dinner, Georgia had told them that her father had been manager of a station very similar to Birraminda, so she had grown up in the outback. Once he had retired, she had gone to the city to find work, but she hadn't been happy and had jumped at the chance to come back. She was friendly and pretty and obviously competent, judging by the way she had rescued the disaster Copper had made of dinner, and the more she had talked, the more inadequate Copper had felt. Georgia could ride and lasso a calf and fly a plane...*and* she was a good five years younger than Copper.

'What a pity you didn't visit your accountant before I turned up here,' she added nastily as she began to get undressed. Mal was stripping off his clothes too, both of them too angry to feel any of the awkwardness that had existed in the past.

'Look, what's the problem?' he demanded. 'You said you had too much work to do and I've found someone to help you. Georgia was free this afternoon, so it made sense to bring her back straight away. I thought you'd be grateful!'

'We do have a phone,' snapped Copper, stepping out of her jeans. 'You might have asked me if I wanted some help!'

Mal swore under his breath as he tossed his shirt aside. 'It never occurred to me that you'd be this unreasonable!'

'I would have liked to have been consulted,' she said stubbornly. 'I *am* supposed to be your wife.'

'Only when you feel like it!'

'Only when *I* feel like it?' Copper echoed incredulously. 'You're the one that treats me like a housekeeper, and not a very satisfactory one at that!'

He restrained himself with an effort. 'I wouldn't have gone to such lengths to find a housekeeper if I thought that's all you were, would I?'

'I don't know.' She peeled off her top and shook her hair irritably out of her eyes. 'It doesn't leave me much to do as a wife, does it? I don't even get to be a wife in bed.'

'And whose fault is that?' said Mal unpleasantly. 'You made it very plain at the time that you only wanted me for that one night. I agreed that I wouldn't touch you unless you asked me to, and you certainly haven't done any asking.'

'A real wife wouldn't have to put in a request,' said Copper, unclipping her bra and reaching for her nightdress. 'Why can't we just behave normally?'

'All right.' Mal walked naked round the bed and twitched the nightdress from her fingers. 'Let's go to bed.'

'*What?*'

'Let's go to bed,' he repeated. 'You want us to be a normal couple. Normal couples make up in bed.'

'Don't be ridiculous,' said Copper tightly, and tried to snatch back the nightdress.

'Oh, no!' said Mal, chucking it out of reach and sweeping her up into his arms to carry her over to the bed, where he dumped her unceremoniously.

The electric shock of his bare flesh against hers had momentarily deprived Copper of speech, and she could only sprawl there as she struggled for breath. Before she could roll away, Mal had pinned her beneath him, her arms outstretched and her green eyes stormy.

'You're the one who wants to be normal,' he reminded her. 'I'll start, shall I?'

The feel of his flesh was indescribably exciting, and Copper's feeble attempts to wriggle out from underneath him only snarled her further in a treacherous tangle of desire. Mal must have felt the instant response of her body, for he released her arms and lifted one of her hands to his mouth instead.

'A normal husband would apologise with a kiss,' he murmured, planting a warm kiss in her palm and then letting his lips move lovingly to her wrist. 'I'm sorry I didn't consult you about employing a new housekeeper,' he went on as his mouth traced a delicious path over the soft skin of her inner arm, nuzzling into the shadow of her elbow before drifting on along her shoulder, lingering at the wildly beating pulse at the base of her throat and reaching her lips at last. 'I'm very sorry,' he breathed against them, and then he had captured her mouth with his own and there was no more need for words as everything exploded into intoxicating delight.

Copper had forgotten that she had meant to resist. She had forgotten the anger and the jealousy and the terrible tension of the last few weeks. Nothing mattered now but the fire that sparked along her veins and gathered into a flame that melted her bones and ravished her senses, consuming everything but the hunger. She wound her arms around Mal's neck and her lips opened to the sinfully seductive exploration of his tongue as she stretched voluptuously beneath him.

'Now it's your turn,' Mal whispered, smiling against her skin.

It was so wonderful to be able to touch him again, to run her hands over the powerful muscles and luxuriate in the warm, taut flesh. Copper's eyes gleamed greenly and she rolled onto him, exhilarated by her own power over the lean, brown body that lay deceptively quiescent beneath her. 'I'm sorry for being so grumpy and ungrateful,' she said obediently as she began to tease kisses along his jaw.

'How sorry?' said Mal indistinctly.

Her lips moved lower and she smiled. 'I'll show you.'

CHAPTER NINE

COPPER shaded her eyes with her hand and squinted across the yard. Yes, there they were, Megan bobbing up and down beside her father, her small face animated, and Mal, head bent to listen to her, slowing his rangy stride to her short little legs. His expression was hidden beneath his hat but, as if sensing Copper's presence, he glanced up and saw her standing there, and their eyes met with an instinctive smile. He was too far away for Copper to hear what he said, but he must have pointed her out to Megan, who spotted her with a cry of pleasure and came running towards her. Mal followed, still smiling, and Copper's heart turned over as she caught the little girl in a hug.

The last few days had been good ones. The terrible tension between her and Mal had crumbled in the face of the mutual need that had set them afire the night he had brought Georgia home. By day, Mal was as coolly self-contained as ever, but something in him had relaxed and, although he rarely touched Copper in front of the others, when the door closed behind them at night the quiet reserve dropped and he would pull her into his arms and make love to her with a tenderness and a passion that left her vibrant and glowing with joy.

He hadn't said that he loved her, but for the time being Copper was content to leave things as they were. It was hard to believe that Mal could make love to her like that without feeling anything, and she saw no need to force a commitment out of him that he was not ready to give. He had three years to fall in love with her, after all, and if the nights passed as the last ten had done, then he must surely find it hard to resist. Copper was still tingling with the memory of the previous night and her mouth curved in a reminiscent smile as she set Megan down.

'You look very pleased with yourself,' said Mal with mock suspicion. 'What are you thinking about?'

Copper's eyes shone warm and green as she smiled at him. 'Tonight,' she said honestly, and rejoiced to see the blaze of response in his face.

'You're a bad woman,' he said softly, but he smiled too as he drew her towards him for a kiss that was warm and sweet with promise.

It was such a natural gesture that Copper's heart cracked with love for him. Could he be coming to love her already? She felt almost giddy with happiness. Everything was working out perfectly. Mal might not love her yet, but he would, and Megan was blooming into a happy, loving child.

Even Georgia was enjoying her new life. The resentment that Copper had felt at the other girl's arrival had been quickly replaced by real liking. Georgia was natural and friendly and a hard worker. She cheerfully took on the cooking and the more humdrum household tasks, which left Copper more time to spend with Megan or working in the office. She still had plenty to do on the project, but she was waiting for the contractors to set a date, and in the meantime she had taken on more and more of Mal's paperwork. Her business experience stood her in good stead and at least she felt that she was being useful.

Only Brett seemed discontented. Oddly, he had made no attempt to flirt with Georgia, and even seemed to actively dislike her. 'She's too perfect,' he told Copper a few days later when she found him sitting moodily alone on the verandah.

'I thought you'd like her,' said Copper, trying to cajole him out of his mood. 'We're worried about you, Brett! A pretty girl with no attachments and you've hardly said a word to her!'

Brett hunched a shoulder. 'She's not that pretty,' he said sullenly. 'I don't like those cool, competent types.'

'Georgia may be competent, but nobody could call her cool,' Copper objected. 'She's a nice, warm, friendly girl, and I wouldn't blame her if she felt hurt at the way you ignore her. It's not as if there are lots of other people out here for her to talk to.'

'She's the one who's ignoring me,' said Brett. 'She always makes me feel as if I've crawled out from under a stone.' He brooded silently for a moment. 'I don't want her approval anyway,' he went on unconvincingly, but with a flicker of his old self. 'She's not nearly as much fun as you, Copper. And have you noticed how chummy she and Mal are?'

After that, of course, Copper *did* notice. Georgia behaved quite naturally, but Copper's jealous eye discerned rather too much approval in Mal's expression when he looked at the other girl. Georgia's knowledge of station life meant that she always knew what Mal was talking about, too, and she could discuss station matters and breaking horses. She knew about musters and how to make billy tea. She could castrate a calf and rope a cow as easily as she could cook a perfect roast, and it wasn't long before Copper began to feel excluded from their conversations. All *she* could talk about was settling invoices and checking accounts, and nobody was interested in that.

Unable to compete when it came to discussing the day, Copper turned more and more to Brett, who kept pointedly aloof from such station conversation and was more than willing to flirt outrageously with Copper instead. Once or twice Copper caught him watching Georgia with an expression that made her suspect that he had been protesting too much about his dislike of the other girl. She was pretty sure that Brett was harder hit than he wanted to admit. His flirting had a desperate edge that she recognised from her own doomed attempts to disguise how she felt about Mal, and a sense of fellow feeling drew them increasingly together.

Mal didn't say anything at first, but as the evenings passed, and the division between the conversations grew more and more obvious, his jaw acquired a set look, and whenever he glanced at Brett and Copper his mouth turned disapprovingly down at the corners. Copper pretended not to notice. Who was Mal to complain about the way she laughed with Brett, when he spent his whole time monopolising Georgia?

Copper could never put her finger on the moment when the warmth and the fire in her relationship with Mal faded. One day it seemed as if they fell laughing into bed together every night, and the next that the following three years would be spent undressing in tense silence.

'Why are you encouraging Brett to make such a fool of himself over you?' Mal asked one night, after Brett had been particularly obstreperous. They were lying stiffly apart in the dark and the words sounded as if they had been forced out of him.

'I'm not *encouraging* him,' said Copper. 'I'm just talking to him, which is more than you and Georgia ever do.'

Mal snorted. 'You call that display "just talking", do you? It doesn't look much like talking to me!'

'I'm surprised you notice,' Copper snapped back. 'You're always nose to nose with Georgia. I thought you'd forgotten who you were married to!'

'*I'm* not the one who seems to have forgotten,' he said grimly. 'You and Brett are the ones who have decided that you needn't bother about a little thing like a wedding ring!'

Exasperated by his obtuseness, Copper struggled up into a sitting position and snapped on the bedside light. If they were going to argue—as they obviously were—they might as well be able to see each other! 'Brett's not interested in me,' she said. 'It's perfectly obvious that he's in love with Georgia.'

'Brett?' Mal sat up too, at that, and turned to her incredulously. 'Brett's never been in love in his life!'

She gritted her teeth and tried not to let the sight of his bare chest distract her. 'I think he is now.'

'And I suppose being in love with Georgia explains why he spends his whole time hanging over you?' he said, not bothering to hide his sarcasm.

'Of course it does,' said Copper impatiently. 'Georgia hasn't shown any interest in him, so Brett doesn't want her to think that he cares about her, that's all.'

'All this amateur psychology doesn't sound very convincing to me,' sneered Mal. 'What makes you such an expert on love suddenly?'

'I know more than you, anyway,' she retorted. 'You wouldn't recognise love if it got up and punched you in the face!'

'Whereas you have all your experience with Glyn to go on!' he snapped back.

'Yes, I do,' said Copper defiantly. 'It's more than you have, anyway! Glyn and I loved each other.'

'Some love when he couldn't wait to dump you for someone else!'

'At least Glyn was honest about what he felt,' she said furiously. 'He's kind and he cares about me, which is more than I can say for you!'

'Why didn't you fight for him if he was so great?' sneered Mal, and Copper's green eyes flashed.

'I wish I had!'

'Just think,' he taunted her, 'if you'd waited a few more weeks, you could have had him back!'

'It's not too late,' Copper pointed out, so angry by now that she hardly knew or cared what she was saying. 'Ellie's still with her husband.'

Mal's brows snapped together. 'How do you know that?'

'There is a world outside Birraminda, you know,' she said sarcastically, 'and I still communicate with it occasionally!'

'You've been in touch with Glyn?' Mal shot out a hand to grasp Copper's arm and pull her round, but she jerked herself out of his grip, terrified in case the mere touch of his fingers against her skin should be enough to defuse her anger. After the numb misery of those endless tense, silent nights, it was oddly invigorating to feel the fury churning through her.

'What if I have? It's none of your business, anyway!'

'None of my business if my wife rings up her ex-lover for cosy little chats? Of course it's my business!'

'We agreed what sort of marriage we were going to have,' she said with a resentful glance, ostentatiously rubbing her arm where he had gripped her with his hard fingers. 'It was to be a purely practical arrangement. There was nothing in the contract about giving up all contact with the outside world!'

'We *agreed* that we would do our best to make sure that everyone thought that we were genuinely married,' said Mal savagely. 'You married me, Copper, and I think it's time you did a better job of acting like my wife than you've done so far—and for a start you can forget all about Glyn until your three years is up!'

Copper shook her hair angrily away from her face. 'Careful, Mal!' she said provocatively. 'You're sounding almost jealous, and you don't want that, do you? Jealousy is one of those "messy" emotions, like love or need, and we all know how you feel about those!'

'What would you know about emotions?' he said unpleasantly. 'All you care about is business.'

'That's good coming from a man who had to resort to blackmail to get a wife!'

'Then I got what I deserved, didn't I?' said Mal with dislike. 'A woman prepared to sell herself just to be able to pitch a few tents and make people pay through the nose for the privilege of sleeping in them!'

Copper's hands clenched around the sheet. 'If that's what you think of me, I think we'd better put an end to this farce right now,' she said, in a voice that shook with fury. 'There's no point in us carrying on like this. All you wanted was a housekeeper, and you've got Georgia now. It's pretty obvious that you think she's doing a much better job than I ever could, so I might as well leave you both to it and go back to Adelaide.'

'What, and give up on your precious project?' Mal mocked. 'You'd never do that, would you, Copper? No, you signed a contract that committed you to staying here for three years, and three years you're going to stay. You can't tear up our agreement just because you've got the chance to go running back to Glyn.'

'It might be worth losing the project to live with a man who appreciated me!' said Copper wildly.

There was a dangerous pause. '*I'd* appreciate you if you'd just stick to your part of our agreement and act like a proper wife,' said Mal, in a voice of cold control. 'And leave Brett alone, of course.'

Back to square one! Copper blew out a hopeless sigh and put her head between her hands. It might have felt good to let off steam, but the argument wasn't going anywhere. 'Look, I keep trying to tell you,' she said grittily. 'Brett only flirts with me because he's jealous of you.

'*Brett's* jealous of *me*?' Mal gave a mirthless laugh. 'That's a good one! How do you work that out?'

'He never gets a chance to impress Georgia because you're always there.' She lifted her head from her hands and tried to explain. 'You're the one who runs everything. You're the one who decides what should be done. You're the one who monopolises Georgia every night. How can Brett compete with you?'

'He's never found any difficulty before!'

'I know, but it's different now. This time Brett's in love.'

'Which he shows by behaving as if he's infatuated with my wife?' Mal suggested sardonically.

Copper gave a despairing gesture. 'It's all aimed at Georgia,' she insisted. 'Surely you can see that?'

'The only thing I can see is you making big green eyes at him every night,' he said in a biting voice as he lay down again and punched his pillow savagely into shape. 'If you left him alone, he might have a chance to fall in love with Georgia, but as it is you're just causing trouble. It's embarrassing for me and extremely awkward for Georgia to see the way you and Brett carry on.'

'Oh, and we can't have *Georgia* feeling awkward, can we?' flared Copper, wrenching the sheet over to her side of the bed before throwing herself angrily down onto her pillow with her back to Mal.

Mal pulled the sheet back. 'I'm warning you, Copper,' he said dangerously. 'You leave Brett alone. I won't stand by and watch you screw my brother up.'

Copper was so enraged that she jerked round to face him. 'All I've done to your brother is to offer him a bit of sympathy and understanding, which is more than he ever gets from you. You're so pig-headed and arrogant that you can't even see what's going on under your own nose!'

'You're not here to understand Brett,' said Mal callously. 'You're here to behave as my wife whenever anybody else is present, and that means not making an exhibition of yourself with my brother—or anyone else. I'd be grateful if you'd remember that in future.'

'You needn't worry,' said Copper in a voice that shook. 'I've got no intention of forgetting why I married you!' Oh, God, the light was still on! Scowling furiously to stop herself from crying, she heaved herself up once more to click it off and then pointedly turned her back. There was a pause, then with a short, exasperated sigh he did the same, and although she lay tensely awake for hours he made no move to touch her again.

It was such a stupid argument, Copper thought wearily the next day. It wouldn't have been too difficult to make up in each other's arms as they had done before. All she had needed to do was to roll over and whisper his name, but part of her had rebelled. Why should she grovel to Mal when she had nothing to apologise for? She wasn't the one being stubborn and blind and completely unreasonable, was she?

'We'll be out mustering all day,' Mal said brusquely at breakfast. 'I need Georgia to spot the strays from the plane, so you'll have to forget your business for once and keep an eye on Megan for a change.'

He clearly thought that was all she was good for, thought Copper, too weary after a sleepless night even to object to his implication that she didn't spend almost all of her time with Megan anyway while Georgia dealt with more of the household chores. She couldn't fly a plane, like Georgia, or ride out with the stockmen, cracking whips and chivvying the cattle along with piercing yells. As far as Mal was concerned, she was useful only for staying at home and keeping out of the way. It was amazing that he hadn't jumped at her suggestion that she go back to Adelaide. After last night, she would have thought he would be glad to be rid of her.

The homestead felt horribly empty when Georgia and the men had gone and Copper was left alone with Megan. Miserably, she began clearing up the kitchen, but the silence was oppressive and accusing and in the end she could bear it no longer. 'Let's have a picnic,' she said to Megan, wanting only to get away from the house with its taunting memories of Mal: Mal climbing the verandah steps, Mal turning his head, Mal closing the bedroom door with a smile in his eyes. 'We'll take my car and go somewhere different for a change.'

Copper hadn't used her car since she had driven up from Adelaide all those weeks ago, and it felt strange getting into it again. The last time she had sat behind the wheel Mal had been just a treasured memory, no more than an image from the past or a vague regret, and now…now he was so much part of her life that it was hard to imagine a time when she had existed without him. To Copper it seemed as if her whole life had been directed to the moment when she had driven up along the track and parked in front of the homestead. It was odd, looking back, to think that she had sat down to wait on the verandah steps without an inkling that Mal would walk around the corner of the woolshed and change her life again for ever.

She thought about how much had changed since then as she drove out along the rough track that led towards a wild, rocky area that she had never seen for herself. Mal had pointed it out once on one of their afternoon rides. It had been too far for them to go on horseback, but he had told her about the eerie red rocks and the spindly gums and the huge termite hills that gave the place its own special atmosphere.

Just remembering those rides made Copper's heart ache for the way things had been then. He had sat on his horse, relaxed and still, and the huge, empty horizon and the dazzling light had focused around him. Then, everything had seemed possible. She hadn't known how contemptuous his eyes could be, or how savage his tongue. Had she changed, or had he?

It took much longer than she had expected to coax

the car along the track, but they made it eventually and ate their picnic in the shade of an overhanging rock. It was a strange, wild place, that echoed with age and silence, but Copper was glad that she had come. Idly, she watched Megan playing house amongst the weirdly shaped stones. The stillness seemed to seep through her, calming her jagged nerves, and she was able to think clearly at last.

She and Mal had been happy before, and they could be happy again. There was no point in hanging onto her pride if it just made her miserable. She would talk to Mal tonight and tell him that she loved him. He might recoil, but at least it would be the truth. Copper didn't think she could bear the thought of spending three years pretending that she cared more for her business than she did for him.

She had to do *something*, anyway. They couldn't go on like this, letting stupid misunderstandings tangle themselves up into bitter arguments. The desire they had felt together was too strong, surely, to fall apart in a matter of days. Copper thought about the way Mal had kissed her and hope twisted inside her. If they could just have a night alone together everything would be all right again. It had to be.

Suddenly eager to get back and tell Mal exactly how she felt, Copper got to her feet and stretched. 'Come on, Megan, let's go home.'

It took a little while to persuade Megan to leave the little house she had created, but at last she was in the car, the picnic was packed away, and she settled herself behind the wheel. Her mind on Mal and what she would say when she saw him, Copper didn't register at first that the engine was wheezing and coughing. When she did, she frowned irritably and tried turning the ignition key again. Nothing happened.

Copper tried again—and again, exasperated, then angry, and at last afraid. Trying to conceal her sinking heart, she got out of the car to open the bonnet and peer helplessly at the engine. She had no idea where to start finding out what was wrong, let alone how to fix it.

The heat bounced off the metal and glared into her eyes. 'I'm hot!' Megan complained.

Biting her lip, Copper opened the door. 'Play in the shade for a while,' she suggested, and went back to the engine. Nothing seemed to be broken. She checked the water and the oil, more for something to do than anything else, and then went to try the ignition again in the wild hope that wishful thinking was enough to do the trick.

It wasn't, of course. Copper wiped her brow with the back of her arm and told herself there was no need to worry. When the muster got back, Mal would realise they were missing and come and find them. He won't know where to look, a cold voice whispered, and ice trickled down Copper's spine before she clamped down on the thought. Mal would find them. All she had to do was sit tight and keep Megan safe.

Megan. Copper got out of the car. Where *was* Megan? Around her were rocks and trees and utter, utter quiet, but no little girl. 'Megan?' Her voice bounced eerily off the stones and her heart seemed to freeze in her chest. 'Megan?'

All at once the afternoon had taken on a nightmarish quality. It was as if she had turned round and found herself on a different time plane, where nothing made any sense. Megan had been there only a minute ago. How could she be gone?

Copper forced herself to breathe deeply and slowly. The one thing she must not do was panic. Calling Megan's name, she began making systematic circles around the car, spreading a little wider every time, until a cry, abruptly cut off, sent her stumbling through the trees in its direction, her heart pounding with dread. Copper found that she was praying as she looked desperately around her for any sign of the child, but she made herself work steadily between the trees until she came out into a sort of clearing and saw Megan, lying sprawled and much, much too still, beneath a weathered red boulder.

'Megan!' Copper fell frantically to her knees beside her. The world had gone suddenly black. 'Please, no…please, no…please, no…' She could hear a voice muttering incoherently, and it was some time before she realised that it was her own and could fight her way back through the darkness to feel for Megan's pulse—a feeble beat that told her the child was unconscious but alive.

'Oh, thank God!' The tears streamed unheeded down Copper's face as Megan stirred and moaned.

'My foot hurts!'

Copper's first reaction was one of relief that it was only her foot. Very gently, she checked Megan all over. One ankle was badly swollen, but she didn't know enough to tell whether it was broken or just sprained. 'What happened, Megan?' she asked.

'I heard you calling, and I was going to hide up on the rocks, but I fell.' Megan began to cry. 'My head hurts as well,' she wept.

She must have hit it as she fell onto the hard ground.

Looking up at the smooth surface of the boulder, Copper went cold. It was quite a drop, and she could have been much more badly hurt. 'It's all right,' she soothed the child, gathering her into her arms without jarring the sore ankle.

Why, why, why had she never learnt any first aid? Megan didn't seem to have hurt anything other than her foot, but who knew what damage the fall might have done to her head? 'Shh,' she murmured into the dark curls, rocking her gently for comfort. She suspected that Megan was more shocked by her fall than anything else, but she might so easily be wrong.

Never had Copper felt more inadequate. Pretending that she knew what she was doing, she ripped up part of her shirt to make a bandage and tied it around Megan's ankle, but the slightest touch was enough to make Megan cry out in pain. 'I want to go home,' she sobbed.

It was only then that Copper remembered the car. 'We can't go home just yet, sweetheart,' she said with difficulty. 'But I'll carry you back to the car and we'll get you some water.'

'I don't want any water. I want to go home!'

'I know, I know.' Copper laid Megan down in the shade near the car and used another piece of her shirt to clean the dust from her face. At least she had thought to bring some water with her. It was the only sensible thing she had done today.

All the time she kept up a flow of cheerful talk, so that Megan wouldn't guess how desperately afraid she was, but inside she was desperately trying to calculate how long it would take Mal to realise that they were missing and organise a search. They were mustering in the far paddocks. What if they didn't get back to the homestead until it was almost dark and it was too late to look for them? She didn't want to think what it would be like to spend a night alone out here, with Megan frightened and hurt and only one bottle of water to see them through.

For what seemed like a lifetime, Copper sat in the shade, cradling Megan on her lap and distracting her by crooning to her softly or telling her stories until she fell into an exhausted sleep. After that there was nothing to do but wait and watch the minute hand of her watch crawl slowly round. The silence gathered weight with every second that passed. Copper could feel it squeezing the air around her, crushing her until she felt so deafened by it that when she heard the plane at last she thought she was hallucinating.

Lying the sleeping child gently on the ground, she struggled out from under the rock. Yes, there was the plane, flying low over the trees but still some distance away. Copper's first impulse was to shout, until she realised that she would only wake Megan needlessly, so she scrambled into the car instead, to begin frenziedly flashing the headlights.

With an excruciating lack of speed, the plane banked and flew towards her, low enough for Copper to see Georgia gesturing from the cockpit as she talked into the radio. Desperately, Copper pointed to the lifted bonnet of the car to show that it had broken down. Georgia nodded and gave Copper the thumbs-up sign for encouragement. Then she dipped her wings and headed back for the homestead.

For a full minute Copper just stared after her, unable to believe that Georgia had just gone and left them there.

Then reason returned and she realised that there was nowhere for the plane to land among all the rocks. Georgia must have been radioing their position back to Mal. The relief was so overwhelming that Copper had to hold onto the car door for support.

Making her way back to their shelter beneath the rock, she gathered the sleepily whimpering Megan back into her lap. 'It's all right now,' she murmured. 'Dad's coming.'

CHAPTER TEN

THE silence was so complete that Copper heard the crunch of changing gears long before she saw Mal's four-wheel drive, but the light was rapidly fading before the vehicle swung into the clearing, its headlights raking across Copper's useless car. By then she was too stiff and weary to move, and she could only sit helplessly as Mal leapt out and looked anxiously around him.

'We're here,' she tried to call, but her mouth was so dry that it came out as no more than a whisper. It was enough, though, for Mal to swing round and see them huddled beneath their rock.

After that everything was a blur for Copper, interspersed with sudden flashes of terrible clarity—like the look on Megan's face when she saw her father or the way Mal's arms tightened round his daughter with a sort of desperation. Too clear was the whiteness of fear around his mouth, the stony expression in his eyes when he looked at Copper and the terrible silence as he drove them home.

'The explanations can wait,' he said curtly, when she tried to tell him what had happened.

Back at the homestead, Georgia was waiting to help them inside. It was Georgia who knew about first aid and could bandage Megan's ankle properly, Georgia who helped Mal to soothe her and wash her and put her to bed. Copper was left to limp stiffly along to the bedroom, too sick at heart to do anything but sit numbly on the side of the bed with the remnants of her shirt in her hands. It was all her fault. She should never have taken Megan out there, should never have taken her eyes off her.

Her sense of guilt was so great that Copper didn't even try and defend herself when Mal came into the room, shutting the door behind him with an ominous click. 'You realise you could have killed my daughter this afternoon?' he said, dangerously quiet.

Copper flinched as if from a blow, but all she could do was turn her head away. She felt Mal's eyes boring into her as he moved into the room. 'You put her in a car that's not fit to drive outside a city and took her out to the most dangerous part of the property,' he said. He didn't raise his voice, but every word was like a lash from a whip. 'And then you let her wander off on her own and hurt herself badly falling off a rock. You might as well have pushed her off yourself!'

'I'm sorry,' whispered Copper, linking her hands together to stop them shaking.

'Sorry? What's the use of being sorry?' Mal was white with fury. 'How dared you take a risk like that with my daughter's life? You didn't even think to leave a note to say where you were going! If Georgia hadn't come back early and found you missing, you could have been out there all night. If she hadn't radioed me straight away it would have been too late for me to get back to a car. As it was she only just spotted you in time. We could all have spent the night driving around in the dark looking for you!'

'I didn't know the car was going to break down,' said Copper painfully.

'It wasn't broken down,' he said with withering contempt. 'Brett's brought it back already. Anyone with the most basic knowledge of mechanics could have fixed it.'

'I don't know anything about mechanics,' she muttered, looking down at her hands.

'Of course you don't!' She could hear Mal striding savagely around the room. 'You don't know about anything useful and you haven't made any attempt to learn. All you've done is push bits of paper around and make a fool out of me!'

Stung out of her guilt and misery, Copper looked up at last. 'That's not true!'

'Isn't it?' Mal's mouth twisted with distaste. 'God, you'd think I'd have learnt my lesson about unsuitable women, wouldn't you? Lisa was just as useless as you, but even she didn't behave as irresponsibly. She might not have spent much time with Megan, but at least she never exposed her to the kind of danger you did today!'

'Why do you keep marrying unsuitable women, then?' Copper leapt to her feet and flung the torn shirt aside, too hurt and bitter to keep still any longer. 'Have you ever thought that when things go wrong it might be something to do with you? No, of course you haven't!' She answered her own question.

'You'll never find a woman who satisfies you, Mal, because you think marriage is something that can be organised by some stupid contract. You accuse me of being obsessed with business, but you're the one who looks at everything in terms of a deal. You always think about what you're going to get out of a marriage and never about what you're going to share. You never give anything of yourself, do you?' She was shaking as she swept on, green eyes blazing with the injustice of his remarks. 'I used to think that it was because you'd been hurt by Lisa, but now I think it's because you've got nothing *to* give—and even if you had, it wouldn't be worth having!'

Mal took a sharp step towards her, and for a moment she thought he was actually going to hit her, but then he had turned on his heel and was at the door. At the last moment he glanced back at Copper with eyes like ice and a voice that dripped with contempt. 'The reason I don't give anything to you, Copper, is that there's nothing I want from you in return.' And he went out, pulling the door behind him with a final, terrible click.

'Copper, you look awful!' Georgia exclaimed in concern when she saw Copper the next morning. Her face was pinched with exhaustion and the green eyes were blank with misery.

'I'm all right.' Copper managed a wavering smile in spite of the fact that there was an agonising pounding behind her eyes and her heart felt as if it was gripped by talons of ice.

She had spent the night curled in a foetal position on the bed, staring numbly at the wall and too despairing even to cry while Mal's words jeered and echoed remorselessly in her brain. Useless. Irresponsible. Worse than Lisa. She hadn't seen him since he had walked out of the room, but she didn't need to. She knew now exactly what he thought of her, and her belief that they would be able to resolve all their differences in bed seemed hopelessly naïve.

Mal would never forgive her for endangering Megan, and the more Copper thought about it the more she thought he was right. She *was* useless here at Birraminda. She didn't belong and she never would. Mal needed a wife like Georgia, who was everything Copper wasn't. The realisation turned Copper's heart to stone, but she knew what she had to do.

She tried to ignore the other girl's worried look. 'How's Megan?'

'She seems fine apart from her ankle,' said Georgia. 'Children are pretty resilient, but we thought she ought to spend the day in bed, anyway, in case there were any after effects from that bump on the head.'

Copper flinched at that 'we'. She knew that it was unintentional, but Georgia's calm good sense only seemed to reinforce her own uselessness. 'I'll go and see her,' she said dully.

Megan was propped up against a pile of pillows, looking more bored than ill, but her face brightened when she saw Copper, and she was anxious to show off her bandaged foot. 'I've got a sprained ankle,' she said proudly, and then, barely pausing for breath, 'Can you read me a story?'

'Not today, sweetheart.' Copper sat down on the edge of the bed, her throat so tight that it was painful to swallow. 'I've got to go to Adelaide.'

'Can I come?' said Megan eagerly.

She shook her head. 'You've got to stay and look after Dad.'

'When are you coming back?'

Copper hesitated. She had been going to tell Megan that she would only be away a week or so, but wasn't that more cruel than telling her the truth? 'I—I'm not coming back, Megan.' It was one of the hardest things she had ever had to say.

Megan stared at her, blue eyes huge as understanding dawned painfully through her confusion. 'You can't go.'

Copper had dreaded this moment, but the look in the child's eyes was worse than anything she could have imagined. 'Dad said you'd stay.' Her voice rose to a wail and then broke as she began to cry.

'Oh, Megan...' Copper pulled the sobbing child into her arms and rocked her, her own tears pouring down her face and into the soft curls buried into her throat. 'I'm so sorry,' she whispered, knowing that for a little girl like Megan being sorry was not enough. 'But Georgia's here to look after you now, and you like her, don't you?'

'I don't want Georgia,' wept Megan. 'I want you! You said you'd stay for ever!'

'Megan, I—' She broke off, her voice suspended in tears. 'I don't want to go.' She tried again. 'I wish I could stay with you for always.'

'Then why are you going?'

How could she explain to a child of four? 'Megan, you love Dad, don't you?' The dark head nodded mutely and Copper struggled to go on. 'So do I, but he doesn't love me.'

'He does! He does!'

Copper tried to close her ears to the anguish in the child's voice. 'Sometimes, when you love someone, you want them to be happy even if it makes you unhappy, and that's what it's like for me. I think Dad would be happier if I went away.'

'No!' sobbed Megan. 'He wants you to stay!'

Copper held her tightly, kissing the dark curls. 'I don't belong here, Megan,' she said brokenly through her tears. 'But I want you to know that I love you very much. I always will.' She swallowed painfully. 'You'll be a good girl for Dad, won't you?'

Megan didn't answer, only clung to her in desperation as Copper tried to lay her back down in the bed, and in the end Copper had to sit there, crooning softly, until she was so worn out by crying that she fell asleep.

Gently Copper covered Megan with a sheet and smoothed the curls away from the flushed, tearstained little face. She stood looking down at her for a long time while her heart splintered inside her, and then she walked quietly away and closed the door behind her.

'You can't go!' Georgia was aghast when Copper told her she was leaving. 'You're in no state to drive anywhere.'

'I have to.' Copper's face felt numb and she was moving stiffly, like an old woman.

Georgia was obviously distressed. 'Copper, I know you and Mal had an argument last night,' she said awkwardly. 'I saw him come out of your room, and he looked as if the world had just ended. But it was such an awful day, and you were both upset. I'm sure if you could just talk about it you'd be able to work everything out.'

'Mal and I have done enough talking,' said Copper. She felt very weary, although it wasn't yet nine o'clock. 'I don't belong here, Georgia. I can't ride a horse or fix a car or strap up an ankle, and after yesterday it's obvious that I'm not even any good at looking after Megan.'

'None of those things matter,' said Georgia urgently. 'The only thing that matters is that you and Mal love each other. Please stay and talk to him tonight!'

'I can't.' Copper's face was ravaged by tears. She couldn't stand to see the disgust in Mal's eyes again. 'I just can't!'

'But what will I tell Mal when he asks why you've gone?'

Copper picked up her case. She had torn her copy of the contract into two and left the pieces on her pillow. 'You won't need to tell him anything. He'll know why I've gone.'

Georgia was crying as she followed her out to the car. 'I wish you wouldn't go,' she wept as Copper turned to hug her goodbye.

'It'll be better for everyone this way.' Copper choked back her own tears. 'Look after Megan for me, Georgia, and tell Mal...tell him I'm sorry...about everything.'

'I'll put a brochure in the post tonight.' Copper put down the phone and rubbed her aching neck. Had she really used to love working in an office?

Over the last ten days she had struggled to pick up the threads of her old life, but she felt trapped in a dull sense of unreality where only the pain inside her seemed less than a blur. Every day seemed interminable, and when she got to the end of each one, like now, there was only the evening stretching bleakly ahead. In the past Copper had thrived on a frenetic lifestyle, but now she hated everything about the city. She hated the tarmac roads and the smell of cars. She hated the endlessly ringing phone and the hours spent making bookings or stuffing brochures into envelopes.

Copper lifted a pile of booking forms and then dropped them listlessly back onto her desk. All she was doing was pushing pieces of paper around, just as Mal had said. Once the very sound of exotic destinations like Quito or Kampala or Rangoon had been enough to thrill her, but now there was only one place she wanted to be.

Birraminda. Copper wanted the empty outback sky, the sharp light and the space and the scent of dust and dry leaves along the creek. She wanted the cockatoos squawking and screeching in the trees and the horses grazing peacefully in the paddock. She wanted the clatter of the screen door and the glare of the sun on the corrugated iron roof and Megan snuggling into her side for a story.

And Mal.

Copper ached with the need to hear his footsteps on the verandah, to watch him settle his hat on his head. She craved the lean, muscled grace of his body and his slow, sure hands on her skin. Most of all she wanted him to fold her in his arms and tell her that he loved her, to melt the ice around her heart and let her live again.

It had taken some time to persuade her parents that she really had left Mal. 'But we were so sure that you were right for each other,' her mother had said, bewildered when Copper had arrived, grey with misery and exhaustion.

'It was all just a pretence,' said Copper bitterly. 'We were just acting.'

Dan Copley snorted. 'If that was acting, you should both be in Hollywood!'

In the end, she had to tell them about the deal she had made with Mal. Her father's face darkened as he heard her story, and Copper felt crushed by guilt at the knowledge that she had thrown his dream away.

'I'm sorry, Dad,' she stammered. 'I know how much you wanted the project at Birraminda, but I'm sure I'll be able to find somewhere else if I—'

'The project!' Dan dismissed his dream with an angry

gesture. 'What does the project matter? All I care about is you! I've a good mind to ring that Mal up right now and give him a piece of my mind! How could he have blackmailed my daughter!'

Seeing that he was working himself up into a state, Copper clutched at his arm and tried to calm him before he put too much strain on his heart. 'Dad, don't! It wasn't blackmail. I chose to marry Mal.'

'He must have forced you. How could you have chosen to marry a man you were only pretending to love?'

Copper's face twisted. 'But I wasn't pretending, Dad. That was the trouble.'

Although still doubtful, her parents had eventually accepted her decision to come home and Copper had thrown herself into work at the office. Anything was better than sitting at home waiting for the phone to ring, or for a knock at the door that would mean Mal had come to find her. He must realise that she had gone back to her parents, but he had made no effort to get in touch with her. This time he had no excuse for not knowing where to find her.

If Mal had loved her, he would have come straight down to Adelaide to fetch her back. At the very least he would have rung to check that she was safe and hadn't broken down again in the middle of the outback. But there had been no word from him at all. That meant that Copper was just going to have to learn to live without him. She had got over Mal once before, she tried to tell herself, and she would again.

With a sigh, Copper pushed back her chair. Six o'clock. Her father would be here any minute. Her car was in for a service and he had promised to come and pick her up. Dully, she switched on the answering machine and straightened the papers on her desk before running her hands wearily through her hair. The vitality that had always been so much a part of her had been drained by despair, and she didn't need to look in the mirror to know that her terrible sense of desolation could be read in her thin face and the green eyes that were smudged with exhaustion.

Outside the window, Copper saw her father's car slide to a halt and she raised a hand in acknowledgement. Locking the door behind her, she went over and got into the car, summoning a smile as she turned to thank her father.

But he wasn't there.

Mal was.

Copper's heart stopped and all the air went whooshing from her lungs as the world tilted alarmingly around her. Mal was *there*, quiet and contained and unbelievably real. He was wearing his moleskin trousers and a dark green shirt open at the throat, and there was an expression in his eyes that Copper had never seen there before. She might even have thought that it was anxiety if her gaze hadn't dropped to the piece of paper sticking out of his shirt pocket.

Copper recognised that paper all too well, and cold, cruel reality wiped out that first dazzling moment of joy with a brutality that clutched agonisingly at her throat. Mal had brought the contract with him and was going to try and force her to its terms.

Bitterness closed around her. There had been times when she had thought that it would be enough just to see him again, but she hadn't wanted it to be like this. 'What are you doing in Dad's car?' she asked him through stiff lips. It was the first thing that came into her head, and even as she asked the question she thought how irrelevant it was.

'He lent it to me.' Calmly, Mal put on his indicator, glanced over his shoulder and pulled out into the traffic. 'Did you think I had stolen it?'

'You've been to see my parents?'

He was concentrating on driving, not looking at her. 'I got here earlier this afternoon. I had to endure an unpleasant session with your father, but once I'd had a chance to explain what I was doing here he gave me the car and told me to come and pick you up myself.'

'And what *are* you doing here?' Copper cast a bitter glance at the contract. 'As if I don't know!'

'I would have thought it would be obvious, yes,' said Mal. 'We need to talk.'

She looked out of the window. How could he sit there, coolly manoeuvring through the traffic, when her world was reeling? 'We've said everything we had to say,' she said bleakly.

'I haven't,' he said.

'Well, I have!'

'That's all right,' said Mal. 'You can listen.'

He drove her to the beach and parked the car facing the sea. Copper felt curiously detached, too shaken by Mal's unexpected appearance even to wonder how he knew the way. It had been a sunny day, but not particularly warm for late summer, and the beach was almost empty—except for an occasional jogger and a few seagulls squabbling over scraps, their cries drifting on the sea breeze.

For a while they sat there without speaking, watching the waves rippling against the sand. Mal seemed to have forgotten that he wanted to talk to her. He was staring through the windscreen, his hands resting on the steering wheel and his shoulders tense.

'Well?' said Copper eventually. 'What is it that you want to say?'

'I wanted to know why you left without saying good-bye.'

'You must know why I left,' she said bitterly. 'You made it very clear what you thought of me the night before and I thought you'd be glad to find that I'd gone.'

Mal turned at that. 'You thought I'd be glad to come home and find that my wife had walked out on me?'

'But I wasn't ever really your wife, was I, Mal?' said Copper. 'Oh, I know we went through a ceremony, and said all the right words in the right places, but it takes more than that to be married. I was only ever a house-keeper as far as you were concerned, and I knew you'd replaced plenty of those before. You didn't even have to go to the trouble of ringing up the agency when you had Georgia there, on the spot, ready to take my place. Why don't you try and blackmail *her* into marrying you? She'd be a far better wife than I ever was!'

Mal half smiled. 'She's certainly ideal—' he began, but Copper couldn't bear to hear any more. She jumped out of the car, blinded by tears, and began to stumble towards the beach. But Mal was cutting her off from the other side.

'Don't you walk away from me again!' he shouted. 'Why do you think I came down here to find you?'

'I don't know!' She tried to brush the tears angrily from her eyes but they kept spilling over. 'I suppose you're going to try waving that contract at me. What are you going to do, sue me for breach of promise?'

'No.' Mal pulled it from his pocket. 'I did bring the

contract with me, though. Look, here it is,' he said, and then, very deliberately, he tore it into tiny pieces. The lightest of breezes lifting off the sea caught them and they fluttered away, to be pounced on by a seagull who carried it away, screeching in triumph.

Copper stared blankly across the bonnet, her tears forgotten. 'That was the contract!' she said stupidly.

'Not any more.'

'But...don't you want it?'

'I never wanted it,' he said.

'But you insisted on it! You only ever opened your mouth to quote it at me! Why would you do that if you didn't want it?'

'God, wasn't it obvious?' cried Mal in sudden despair. 'I did it because it was the only way I could make you stay!'

The words rang between them, echoing in the sudden silence. Copper couldn't move. She could only gaze at Mal in disbelief as he walked round the front of the car to take her very gently by the elbows.

'I never wanted the contract, Copper,' he said. 'I only ever wanted you.'

'Y-you wanted a housekeeper,' she corrected him. She was trembling, terrified of facing the bitterness of disillusion again but incapable of ignoring the hope that was flickering into life against all the odds.

'I told myself that, but it was only an excuse. I'd been looking for one ever since I looked across the yard and saw you sitting on the steps next to Megan.' His thumbs moved tantalisingly over her inner arms, caressing the soft skin. 'It was like a miracle, to find you again after seven years.'

'I didn't think you even remembered me,' said Copper

unsteadily. 'You can't tell me that you'd been waiting for me all that time!'

'I hadn't been waiting, no,' said Mal, 'but I had been regretting. I'd accepted that I would never see you again, and then I met Lisa. I wanted her to make me feel the way you had done, but she could never be you and the marriage was a disaster from the start. I can't tell you how many times I'd find myself thinking about you, about the way you smiled, the way you closed your eyes when I kissed you, the way you felt in my arms.'

He paused, looking down into Copper's face, and the expression in his eyes made her heart beat faster. 'I used to wonder what my life would have been like if my father hadn't died just then, or if you'd been in when I called, but I knew there was no point in wishing that things had been different, so I tried my best to forget you. And then, just when I thought I'd managed to push you to the back of my mind, suddenly there you were.'

'Why didn't you tell me this then?' she asked uncertainly, and Mal's fingers tightened around her arms.

'I wasn't sure that the time we'd spent together in Turkey had meant the same thing to you. You'd obviously got on with enjoying your life and you didn't seem to have any regrets.' His mouth twisted. 'And Lisa taught me to be wary. It was a blow to realise that you were so determined about your business, but I thought that if I could just get you to stay a little longer we'd have a chance to get to know each other again. When you offered to stay on as housekeeper it seemed too good to be true, but it wasn't long before I realised that wasn't going to be enough. You'd made it clear that your business was your priority, and I knew you wouldn't stay just because I asked you.'

'So you thought you'd try a spot of blackmail?' said Copper, with the beginnings of a smile.

Mal grimaced. 'It was all I could think of, but it just made things worse. I felt guilty at having forced you into a marriage that you didn't want, and the very fact that you'd agreed made it obvious that your business meant far more to you than I ever could.'

Could he really have been so blind? 'Did it seem like I was thinking of business on our wedding night?' she asked, and he slid his hands slowly up her arms.

'I wasn't sure,' he confessed. 'When I made love to you, I was sure that you had to feel the same, but I'd watched you with Glyn at the wedding, and I remembered what you'd said about still loving him. I was afraid you'd just been trying to forget him, and when I woke up the next morning and saw the contracts I realised what an impossible situation I'd put us both in. I knew that I'd no right to touch you unless you asked, because that's what I'd agreed, but you've no idea how hard it was to lie next to you night after night.'

'Don't I?'

She smiled at him as she spoke and Mal gripped her shoulders. 'Copper,' he said with sudden urgency. 'I've said a lot of stupid things about love. I pretended that I didn't want anything more to do with it after Lisa, when all the time I was just afraid to tell you how much I loved you. I came down because I knew I had to apologise for the way I treated you, but all I really want is to ask you to come back.'

He hesitated, and Copper marvelled at the uncertainty in his expression. 'I've got no right to ask you, I know, but Birraminda isn't the same without you. It isn't like before. You're not just a special memory any more. I *need* you now, and Megan needs you too.' He gestured at the scattered pieces of paper. 'The contract doesn't exist any more. I want you to come back because *you* want to, not because some lawyer says you have to.'

His hands cupped her face lovingly and his voice was very low. '*Will* you come back, Copper? Not as a housekeeper, not as a wife—not as anything but yourself?'

Copper slipped her arms around his waist and smiled up at him with shining eyes. 'It depends how long you want me to stay this time.'

'Nothing less than for ever will do,' said Mal.

'For ever it is, then,' she said, and melted joyously into his kiss. He crushed her against him, kissing her with a deep, desperate hunger, and Copper clung to him, dizzy with pleasure and almost aching with the happiness of knowing that he loved her.

'Are you sure you want me back?' she asked much later, struck by sudden doubt as they walked slowly along the beach together. 'I'm so hopeless at everything. I can't do any of the things your wife should be able to do. You need someone who knows what they're doing and—'

Mal stopped her with another long kiss before she could say any more. 'I need *you*,' he said against her mouth. 'Only you.'

Deeply satisfied, Copper wound her arms around his neck and nibbled tiny, tantalising kisses along his jaw. 'But I thought Georgia was your ideal wife,' she murmured provocatively into his ear.

'*If* you'd let me finish,' said Mal, 'you'd have heard me say that Georgia was the ideal wife for Brett.' He pretended to sound stern, but she could feel his cheek crease into a smile beneath her lips. 'You were right about that too, which just goes to show how useful you're going to be.'

'Georgia and Brett are getting married?' Copper pulled back at the news, delighted. 'When did that happen?'

'After you left. Trying to cope with me brought them together—I think it made them realise how they'd feel if one of them left.'

'I knew Brett was in love, but I didn't realise Georgia felt anything for him!' Copper tucked herself into Mal's side as they resumed their walk.

'I don't think she wanted to be just another girl for him, so she held off as long as she could,' Mal told her. 'She's certainly the only girl Brett's ever taken seriously, and I think she'll be good for him. He's steadier already. I've been so taken up with running around after you that he's had to take over a lot of the work on the station, and it's done him the world of good. There's a nice property up for sale not too far away, and together they should make a success of it.' He smiled down at Copper. 'They're just waiting for you to come back so that they can get married.'

Copper flashed him a demure look from beneath her lashes. 'So you're not jealous of Brett any more?'

'Not now,' said Mal with a rueful smile. 'I was, though. But not nearly as jealous as I was of Glyn. I kept thinking about the things you'd said about him— how he was kind and honest and a good friend—and I was terrified that you'd decide to go back to him. And later, when I thought about the things I'd said to you, I didn't think I could blame you.'

His arms tightened. 'I said some unforgivable things to you that last night, Copper,' he confessed. 'I've never been as scared as I was when I heard that you and Megan were missing, but I was still angry after that argument the night before and I took it all out on you. It didn't help, though, and I felt so bad the next day that I turned back halfway out to the muster. I was going to tell you that I was sorry, and hadn't meant what I'd said, but when I got back Georgia had to tell me you'd gone.'

The memory made Mal crush her so hard against him that she could hardly breathe, but Copper didn't mind. 'It was the worst moment of my life,' he said. 'Georgia was crying, Megan was inconsolable, Brett kept telling me what a bloody fool I'd been—but all I could think was that you'd decided to try and work things out with Glyn after all. I remembered what you'd said about it not being too late now that Ellie was back with her husband, and I was so desperate and angry at first that I refused to go after you. I've spent the last ten days in hell, imagining you with him, and this morning I couldn't stand it any longer. I flew down and went straight to your parents', but you weren't there. Your father tore a strip off me for making you so unhappy, but when I told him that my life just wasn't going to be worth living unless I could persuade you to come back and try again, he took pity on me and tossed me the car keys!'

'Mal?' Copper held herself slightly away from him so that she could look deep into his eyes. 'Have I told you that I love you?'

He smiled at her in a way that made her heart sing. 'Now that you come to mention it, I don't think you have,' he said.

'I do,' said Copper, and kissed him—a long, warm,

inexpressibly sweet kiss that thrilled with the promise of the years to come.

Later, much later, they took off their shoes and walked barefoot along the sand. It was cool and soft between Copper's toes and reminded her of the beach they had walked along seven years ago, hand in hand as now but knowing nothing then of the long road that would bring them back together again.

'We don't have to get married again now that we've torn up our contracts, do we?' she murmured, nuzzling Mal's throat as they halted for yet another kiss.

'We don't need another wedding, but I think we might have another honeymoon, don't you?' said Mal. 'Why don't we tell your parents that the project's on again, and then take ourselves back to that hotel in the hills? We could have a real honeymoon now that we don't need to pretend any more.' His lips drifted along Copper's jaw to linger at her mouth. 'How does that sound?'

Copper heaved an ecstatic sigh as they turned towards the car. 'It sounds like heaven!'

Three days later, the little plane flew over the creek and touched down at Birraminda. 'Welcome home,' said Mal, leaning over to kiss Copper as they came to a bumpy halt.

Brett and Georgia were waiting together on the edge of the landing strip, restraining an impatient Megan with difficulty until the propeller had spun to a stop. But as Mal lifted Copper down, his hands hard and possessive at her waist, she came flying over the dust towards them.

'Copper, Copper!' she called, and flung herself into Copper's waiting arms. 'You came home!'

Copper lifted her up in a tight hug, and the green eyes that met Mal's over the small head shone with love. 'Yes,' she said. 'I'm home now.'

MILLS & BOON®

Next Month's Romances

♡

Each month you can choose from a wide variety of romance novels from Mills & Boon. Below are the new titles to look out for next month from the Presents™ and Enchanted™ series.

Presents™

PERFECT MARRIAGE MATERIAL	Penny Jordan
LOVESTRUCK	Charlotte Lamb
A MARRIAGE TO REMEMBER	Carole Mortimer
A VERY PUBLIC AFFAIR	Sally Wentworth
RECKLESS ENGAGEMENT	Daphne Clair
CHRISTMAS WITH A STRANGER	Catherine Spencer
A FRAGILE MARRIAGE	Rosalie Ash
THE GROOM'S REVENGE	Kate Walker

Enchanted™

THE COURTING CAMPAIGN	Catherine George
TEMPORARY HUSBAND	Day Leclaire
NO WIFE REQUIRED!	Rebecca Winters
BABY IN THE BOARDROOM	Rosemary Gibson
DO YOU TAKE THIS COWBOY?	Jeanne Allan
KISSED BY A STRANGER	Valerie Parv
RAINY DAY KISSES	Debbie Macomber
EXPECTATIONS	Shannon Waverly

MILLS & BOON®

Christmas Treats

**A sparkling new anthology
—the perfect Christmas gift!**

Celebrate the season with a taste of love in this
delightful collection of brand-new short stories
combining the pleasures of food and love.

Figgy Pudding
by PENNY JORDAN
All the Trimmings
by LINDSAY ARMSTRONG
A Man For All Seasonings
by DAY LECLAIRE

And, as an extra treat, we've included the
authors' own recipe ideas in this
collection—because no yuletide would be
complete without...Christmas Dinner!

MISSING LINKS

How would you like to win a year's supply of Mills & Boon® books? Well you can and they're FREE! Simply complete the competition below and send it to us by 30th April 1998. The first five correct entries picked after the closing date will each win a year's subscription to the Mills & Boon series of their choice. What could be easier?

1. APPLE	P I E	CRUST
2. STRAWBERRY	_ _ _	TARTS
3. MINCED	_ _ _ _	BALLS
4. PICKLED	_ _ _ _ _	RING
5. GRAPE	_ _ _ _ _	JUICE
6. FRENCH	_ _ _ _ _	SAUCE
7. TOFFEE	_ _ _ _ _	CRUMBLE
8. PEANUT	_ _ _ _ _ _	BEANS
9. TANDOORI	_ _ _ _ _ _ _	CURRY
10. PRAWN	_ _ _ _ _ _ _ _	SAUSAGES

Please turn over for details of how to enter ⇨

C7J

HOW TO ENTER

There are ten missing words in our list overleaf. Each of the missing words must link up with the two words on either side to make a type of food.

For example, the word *Pie* links with *Apple* and *Crust* to form *Apple Pie* and *Pie Crust*:

APPLE - PIE - CRUST

As you find each one, write it in the space provided, we've done the first one for you! When you have linked up all the words, don't forget to fill in the coupon below, pop this page in an envelope and post it today—you don't even need a stamp!

Hurry, competition ends 30th April 1998.

Mills & Boon® Missing Links Competition
FREEPOST, Croydon, Surrey, CR9 3WZ

EIRE readers send competition to PO Box 4546, Dublin 24.

Please tick the series you would like to receive
if you are a winner:

Presents™ ❑ Enchanted™ ❑ Medical Romance™ ❑
Historical Romance™ ❑ Temptation® ❑

Are you a Reader Service™ Subscriber?   Yes ❑   No ❑

Ms/Mrs/Miss/Mr _____
                                    (BLOCK CAPS PLEASE)
Address_____

_____

_____ Postcode_____

(I am over 18 years of age)   C7J

One application per household. Competition open to residents of the UK and Ireland only. You may be mailed with offers from other reputable companies as a result of this application. If you would prefer not to receive such offers, please tick box.   ❑

Mills & Boon is a registered trademark of
Harlequin Mills & Boon Limited.

Mills & Boon® invite you to a wedding...

...And it could be your own!

On one very special night, single people from all over America come together in the hope of finding that special ingredient for a happy ever after—their soulmate. The inspiration behind The Ball is simple—come single, leave wed. Which is exactly what happens to three unsuspecting couples in

Day Leclaire's
wonderful new trilogy:

Look out for the following books:

November: TEMPORARY HUSBAND
December: ACCIDENTAL WIFE
January 1998: SHOTGUN MARRIAGE

"Day Leclaire ensures a good time will be had by all."
—*Romantic Times*

Get swept away by

RISING
Tides

by award-winning author EMILIE RICHARDS

**The reading of a woman's will threatens
to destroy her family.**

*In this explosive sequel to the critically acclaimed
Iron Lace, family, friends and strangers gather for
the reading of Aurore Gerritsen's will. The threat of
an approaching hurricane becomes a minor incident
as each bequest reveals yet another dark family secret.*

Valid only in the UK & Ireland against purchases made in retail outlets
and not in conjunction with any Reader Service or other offer.

50ᵖ OFF
COUPON
VALID UNTIL: 31.1.1998

EMILIE RICHARDS' *RISING TIDES*

9 904170 190503

0472 00172